Dedalus Original Fiction in Paperback

THE RUNES HAVE BEEN CAST

Robert Irwin (born 1946) is a novelist, historian, critic and scholar. He is a Fellow of the Royal Society of Literature.

He is the author of eight previous novels, all published by Dedalus: *The Arabian Nightmare*, *The Limits of Vision*, *The Mysteries of Algiers*, *Exquisite Corpse*, *Prayer-Cushions of the Flesh*, *Satan Wants Me*, *Wonders Will Never Cease* and *My Life is like a Fairy Tale*.

All of Robert's novels have enjoyed substantial publicity and commercial success although he is best known for *The Arabian Nightmare* (1983) which has been translated into twenty languages and is considered by many critics to be one of the greatest literary fantasy novels of the twentieth century.

Robert Irwin

THE RUNES HAVE BEEN CAST

Dedalus

Published in the UK by Dedalus Limited
24-26, St Judith's Lane, Sawtry, Cambs, PE28 5XE
email: info@dedalusbooks.com
www.dedalusbooks.com

ISBN printed book 978 1 912868 53 7
ISBN ebook 978 1 912868 54 4

Dedalus is distributed in the USA & Canada by SCB Distributors
15608 South New Century Drive, Gardena, CA 90248
email: info@scbdistributors.com   web: www.scbdistributors.com

Dedalus is distributed in Australia by Peribo Pty Ltd
58, Beaumont Road, Mount Kuring-gai, N.S.W. 2080
email: info@peribo.com.au   web: www.peribo.com.au

First published by Dedalus in 2021

Printed and bound in the UK by Clays, Elcograf S.p.A
Typeset by Marie Lane

A C.I.P. listing for this book is available on request.

Should any of my readers incline to a serious study of the subject of this book, and thus come in contact with a Man or Woman of Power, I feel that it is only right to urge them, most strongly to refrain from being drawn into the practice of the Secret Art in any way. My own observations have led me to an absolute conviction that to do so would be a complete waste of time.

CHAPTER ONE

'Procul hinc, procul este, severae!'
'Stay far hence, far hence, forbidding ones!'
(Ovid, *Amores*.)

Although Lancelyn owed (if 'owed' was the right verb) his first experience of the apparently supernatural to a tin of alphabet spaghetti, his introduction to the theory and literature of hauntings had come a couple of years earlier. It was an evening in the eighth week of Michaelmas Term 1960. It must have been in early December then. Their tutor Mr Edward Raven had set them both an essay on the Victorian ghost story. Bernard was as annoyed as Lancelyn was, since time was running out and in May they would be sitting finals and the chances of an essay question on how spectres managed to comport themselves in Victorian literature was negligible. They ought to have been doing something on somebody major, Browning, Thackeray or Gaskell. But Raven never paid much attention to the syllabus and he set little stock on the apparent need of undergraduates to get good degrees, for Oxford was not to be thought of as a kind of sausage machine for producing degree-bearing students.

Lancelyn had arrived first, a bit breathless, having finished his essay five minutes earlier and he accepted the ritual glass of sherry. Bernard arrived ten minutes later and Raven's eyebrows rose, but only for an instant. He was used to Bernard's lateness and to his coloured waistcoats. But the spats! This was something new. Lancelyn wondered what on earth spats were for. He had read about them in books, but literature gave no guidance on the subject. There were so many subjects on which English literature could give no guidance. The short term *ad hominem* answer was that they, like the coloured waistcoats, were part of the image Bernard had been madly cultivating ever since his first year. Right at the start he put it about that now he was at Oxford he had no other aim than to be elected to the Bullingdon Club. Hence the waistcoats and the preposterous speech mannerisms. This was absurd. Bernard was a grammar schoolboy and God knows how he could have afforded the waistcoats and when his talk was reported to the Bullingdon, some of its members, quite reasonably suspecting that he was taking the mickey, turned up at Merton and trashed his room, but Bernard had emerged from the room seemingly proud of even that much recognition.

Lancelyn read first. His essay was the product of a diligent trawl through the obvious texts by Dickens, Wilkie

Collins, Bulwer-Lytton and Le Fanu. He drew attention to the moralising messages that such stories delivered and in his conclusion (of which he was quite proud) he suggested that the growth in popularity of the ghost story in the nineteenth century was a reaction to the age's rationalism, utilitarianism and industrialisation. Shortly afterwards the antiquarian ghost fictions of M.R. James would usher in a new era of horror.

Raven did not comment, but gestured for Bernard to read his essay.

'Righty ho.'

The essay that Bernard read covered some of the same ground, though 'read' was not strictly the right word since what Bernard 'read' from (and Raven, sitting where he was, could not see this) were several blank sheets of paper. Though Bernard stumbled a couple of times, he apologised and claimed that this was due to an inability to read his own handwriting and, talking fluently as ever, he picked up on several points that Lancelyn had missed. He pointed out the childishness of so many of the ghostly fictions in which goodness was invariably rewarded and wickedness punished, just as in the stories of Enid Blyton. Mostly though he focussed on the importance of ambiguity and uncertainty in some of the writings of Sheridan Le Fanu and in Henry James' *The Turn of the Screw*. He too concluded with Monty James and the way he set so many of his tales in the seventeenth and eighteenth centuries rather than in 'the age of steam and cant'.

Raven did not respond immediately to the essays. Instead, and this was something new, he poured them each a second glass of sherry, before speaking,

'Did you know that our college has a ghost?'

They did not.

'It would be strange if after so many centuries Merton had not acquired a ghost. He has been seen in the upstairs part of the library, where the chained books are, as well as just outside the College walls in Dead Man's Walk. We know who he is – or rather was. He was Colonel Francis Windebank, the son of Charles I's Secretary of State. In 1645 the King put him in charge of Bletchingdon Park. This great house was well fortified and Windebank had a garrison of two hundred men under him. Since he was newly married, he thought to mark the occasion and impress his bride by holding a ball in the place. There were many guests, but before the ball could get under way, Cromwell arrived on one of his raiding parties into Oxfordshire and began to make preparations for a siege of the house. But Windebank, anxious for the lives of his bride and their guests, promptly surrendered to terms. Then he and his bride made their way back to Oxford. There he was promptly arrested and, after a three-hour court martial, he was sentenced to death for cowardice and taken out to Dead Man's Walk to be shot. It was reported that before the firing squad was quite ready, he bared his chest and shouted 'Long live the King!' And so now his apparition occasionally manifests itself along the wall just below Merton's garden and more frequently in the library. It is odd, the affinity that ghosts seem to have for libraries. Why am I telling you all this?... I don't know... yes, I do.'

Raven drained his sherry before continuing, 'You have not been visualising your stories in the way that I taught you and you are both missing something. To start with, people who have seen the ghost of Windebank merely report that they have seen the ghost. They are not gibbering or crazed out of their wits by terror. They have no sense that the ghost has been sent to them to deliver a message or to punish them for curiosity or some unspeakable personal sin. Nor is there any Jamesian ambiguity. (Here I mean Henry James, not M.R.) They have just *seen* the damn thing. The ghost story, on the other hand, aims to induce fear in the reader. That is almost always the main purpose of a ghost story and yet the word 'fear' never appeared in either of your essays. But I suppose you are too young to have experienced real fear… you will … you will. Anyway, in your essays you needed to address the ways in which prose technique and narrative structure can be controlled in such a way as to induce fear. Then, of course, you should have considered the readership and the desire of so many readers to experience fear. Why this need on their part?'

They had no ideas. But soon Raven moved on to other matters and, in particular he queried Lancelyn's argument that the ghost story was a reaction against Victorian rationalism, for surely it was the Victorians' scientific approach to everything that led to the founding of the Society for Psychical Research in 1881 and this had to be seen as evidence of the Victorians' rational drive to understand the mysteries of the unseen.

Afterwards, 'What do you think he meant by saying that we would know fear?'

'Hmm, a bit of a poser that one. Perhaps he was talking about finals. Fancy a drink? Or perhaps he was just trying to put the heebie-jeebies on us.'

'Why should he do that?'

Bernard shrugged, 'A strange man. Fancy a drink?' he asked again.

They went to The Chequers on the High Street and Lancelyn bought the beers.

They talked about Raven's many prejudices, including his hatred of doctorates and research, his contempt for publication (which was rather odd in someone who taught literature) and above all his detestation of Professor Tolkien and his 'bloody elves'. 'If a novelist is ever stuck for what happens next in a plot, all he needs to do is just have another bloody elf come in.' Tolkien thought that English literature came to an end with Chaucer, whereas Raven was certain that true literature only started to appear in the early eighteenth century. But Tolkien was now Emeritus, having retired from the Merton Professorship of Language and Literature in the previous year and nowadays he was only rarely glimpsed making his way across Mob Quad and heading for the library.

The pub was not crowded. There was a young woman in a dark blue sheath dress at the next table along from them, busy writing with her glass of white wine untouched. Though she looked like a student, it was pretty much taboo for female undergraduates to drink alone in pubs.

Bernard and Lancelyn drifted on to talk about life after finals. Was there life after finals? Lancelyn thought that he might become a librarian. Bernard was incredulous.

'A librarian! My hat! Are you sure that you will be safe from real life in a library?'

'It is all my third-class degree will be good for.'

'Don't play the giddy ass! You must know that Raven thinks that we are both brilliant. He just doesn't say so, but that is why we are in the same tutorial. We are both certain to get firsts.' Then, 'How about another drink?'

Lancelyn bought this round too and Bernard made his ritual remark about expecting a postal order any day now from his aunt in India. Lancelyn knew almost nothing about Bernard's real family, but a great deal about the clan of fantasy aunts, one or two of whom were always threatening a visit to Oxford.

Their talk became more general about the future. Bernard was sure he could find a way of not working for a living. Life would be one long lark in which barmaids were kissed, policemen's helmets were stolen and ten pound notes were burned. Lancelyn, on the other hand, did not want the future to happen. He had read Aldous Huxley's *Brave New World* and had been appalled by its prospectus of sex and drugs on demand – on demand and all but compulsory.

Sex was almost as certain as death. He could easily imagine that sexual love would prove to be a far more testing exam than the Oxford finals. But there were so many other uncertainties. Friendships made and lost, emotional and physical pain and, between all that desire and anguish, so very many hours of pure boredom. And there were so many things he would have to tackle for the first time in his life and he had as yet so little experience to draw on with which to tackle them. The prospect of finding his way in a world which did not yet exist terrified him. And finally he would have to learn how to say goodbye to so much beauty. Did it all have to happen? Yes, the future had to be filled somehow.

Bernard was talking about how he would end up comfortably in an old folk's home in one of the domed cities of Mars, when suddenly, and still talking, he leapt from his chair and seated himself opposite the young woman, who, alarmed, stopped writing.

'You have been eavesdropping on us and writing down everything we say. What's going on? Are you by any chance a spy for Mr Raven? How much is he paying you?'

The woman looked uncomfortable and shook her head.

'I am writing a novel,' she said.

'Neither are we,' said Bernard dismissively and gestured for Lancelyn to join them. Lancelyn brought the beers over.

'No, I really am,' she insisted. 'I take my notebook with me and go about on buses and sit in cafes and pubs trying to get it right how people talk and think. I want to write from real life and not copy other people's books.'

Her hair was luxuriant, her face a little plump and her breasts heavy. She was flushed and angry. Also beautiful and she knew it.

Bernard nodded impatiently. Then, 'Eeeh, look! A man in a gorilla suit has just walked in.'

She turned to look and as she did so he snatched her notebook from her. He riffled through the pages until he got to the last two with writing on.

'Yes,' he said. 'She has got most of it down. God! Are we not brilliant? You do not often hear conversations like this on buses. And what's this?' He read out, 'Tall, ash-blonde, brilliant blue eyes, strong chin. That is you, Lancelyn. What about me? There is nothing about me. Oh yes, there is. Just one word. "Spats".'

Disappointed, he pushed the notebook back to her.

'Are you an undergraduate?'

She nodded.

'Where?'

'Somerville.'

'Reading?'

'History.'

'And your name?'

'Molly. Molly Ransom.'

'We will wait for your novel, for years, for decades if necessary. I am Bernard. And this is Lancelyn. We are both at Merton.' He drained his beer. 'And now, Miss Ransom, we must be going. Toodle pip!'

As he rose, he made as if to tip his non-existent hat. Lancelyn, looking apologetic, followed him out.

Outside, Bernard turned to Lancelyn, 'Of course if we had realised that what we were saying was being written down, we might have managed to talk even more brilliantly yet. I am really cheesed off, since anybody can write a novel and anybodies do. But I have always wanted to be a character in a novel. That would really be something – like Leigh Hunt got into Dickens' *Bleak House* as Harold Skimpole and William Henley made it as Long John Silver in *Treasure Island*. That would really be something, to be immortalised in fiction. But that girl is never going to write her novel, and, even if she did, you, not me, would be its hero. You see me downcast and chopfallen. So I could do with another drink.'

That meant repairing to Lancelyn's rooms where he had a bottle of vodka. Just inside the porter's lodge they picked up Marcus, an amiable second-year historian. Then on the way to the room they met Sam Garner, the scout on their staircase, lurking at its foot. He was good at lurking. Bernard paused to ask him, 'Garner, have you ever seen this ghost of a cavalier, Sir Francis Somebody?'

Sam nodded, 'Yes sir, two years ago I saw a man in very old-fashioned costume coming out of the library. Then suddenly he was not there.'

'And you were not frightened?'

'There was no nothing to be frightened of. As I say, he was not there.' And Sam went off to lurk somewhere else.

Once they were inside Lancelyn's room, Bernard commented, 'Real life ghosts are wasted on someone like Sam.'

'Ghosts seem pretty pointless anyway,' said Lancelyn. 'Besides how do we know it is Windebank's ghost? It might be some other cavalier, or the ghost of someone who was up in the 1920s and who went to a fancy dress party.'

'Yes, I like that. A fancy dress party in which identities were mistaken and which ended in a lethal tragedy...' Bernard continued to fantasise in this vein.

Meanwhile Marcus was gazing with wonder at Lancelyn's books. A bookcase covered a whole wall and it was tightly packed and some of the books were bound in leather. There were no paperbacks, but there were many early books on conjuring and other magic, including Thomas Hill's *A Briefe and Pleasaunt Treatise, Intituled Naturall and Artificiall Conclusions*, Reginald Scot's *The Discoverie of Witchcraft*, S.R.'s *The Art of Jugling or Legerdemaine* and the anonymous *Mathematical Recreations*. If Marcus had been invited to Bernard's room, he would have found no books at all except for stuff borrowed from libraries, and no alcohol either.

Lancelyn passed round cigarettes. They were the Black Russian cigarettes that he and Bernard affected.

'That girl we met was quite a popsy-wopsy, wasn't she Lancelyn?'

Lancelyn reflected, Yes, judging the matter objectively, he could see that she had been beautiful. Perhaps a woman out of a Titian painting. No, not Titian. Her hair was too dark and luxuriant and the eyes so large. More Alphonse Mucha. Yes, she would have been perfect for a poster by Mucha. Intimidatingly beautiful then. But Lancelyn said nothing and merely nodded.

'An absolute corker!' Bernard insisted. 'I really think we must pay Somerville a visit, don't you?'

Again Lancelyn said nothing and this time he did not nod. He was damned if he was ever going to set foot in Somerville.

The glasses had been taken away by Sam to be washed and had not yet been returned. So they drank the vodka out of coronation mugs.

Marcus could not see why English literature was a degree. Surely anybody could just read all those novels and poetry in the bath? There was no need to teach one how to read books in the bath. But, if the stuff really was so obscure that it needed to be taught, then it was almost certainly not worth reading. But then perhaps, after all, he too should have read literature. As it was, he was depressed, 'The whole history syllabus is devoted to training us up to be professional historians, but I don't want to be an academic. None of us does. I want to do something in the real world.'

Then looking over to the shelf, 'I envy you your books.'

'But you have lots of books. I have seen them all over the place in your rooms.'

Marcus sighed, 'There are a few history textbooks but most of the rest are about coal mining.'

'We had no idea that you were a bit of a coal buff,' said

Bernard, who was excited to learn this.

Marcus sighed again. (He was rather prone to sighing.)

'I am not, but second-hand books on coal are so very cheap that they are just irresistible. It is very easy to build up a big collection of books on coal. So cheap, it is like stealing sweets from a baby.'

Previously Lancelyn had entertained the notion that historians were more sensible than Eng. Lit. students. He now dropped this idea.

A second round of vodka emptied the bottle.

'And I am sad to find that I am nothing in Molly Ransom's eyes,' said Bernard. 'But hey! We shall all look back on our time at Oxford as the best years of our lives. You will see if I am not right. I now propose a toast.'

What should the toast be to?

Bernard thought for a minute. Then, 'To Professor Tolkien and his bloody elves.'

'Professor Tolkien and his bloody elves!'

'Professor Tolkien and his bloody elves!'

Having swiftly drained his mug, Bernard hurled it back against the wall behind him on which it smashed. Marcus followed suit and his mug did the same. Then Lancelyn threw his mug back. He fleetingly had the sensation of something passing over the bookshelf opposite, perhaps like a hand, but perhaps more like nothing. The next thing he was aware of was Bernard, looking concerned and leaning over him and sprinkling water over his face. Apparently Lancelyn's heavy mug, instead of smashing, had bounced back and hit him on the back of the head and had briefly knocked him out.

Bernard and Marcus, after checking that his head was not

bleeding and that he really was alright, left Lancelyn to his groggy reflections. 'The best years of our lives?' Certainly not. The best years of his life had already passed and they had been at Eton. There was the rowing on the river; the voices of the Eton College Chapel Choir; the Greek dramas performed in their original language; the Eton versus Harrow cricket match; the long walks with handsome and clever youths. 'Are we not men?' Well, not quite. Lancelyn had been a colleger, a fagmaster, a rower and a member of Pop, in short, one of the Lords of Creation. He had come close to crying on his last day at Eton. Nothing would ever be so good again. Thenceforth the Gates of Paradise were guarded with a fiery sword by the Angel of the Past. Oxford was only tolerable as an inferior substitute for Eton. In the same way and soon real life would surely turn out to be an inferior substitute for Oxford.

CHAPTER TWO

A few days later it was the end of the university term. Lancelyn's parents were in New York and they invited him to join them there. He was seriously tempted. The Met would be staging *Nabucco* and *Salome*. But he really needed to work. So instead he went where he would not be disturbed and he booked himself into the Majestic in Cannes and he arrived there with two suitcases, one of which was full of books. They included works by Spenser, Webster, Tourneur, Browne, Burton, Herrick, Donne and De Quincey. But he had also brought along an omnibus volume of M.R. James and a string of thrillers by someone called Fleming. He had first read the M.R. James stories as a schoolboy. It was hard to be at Eton and not be aware of the scary stories produced by its former Provost, but the Fleming stuff was new to him and it turned out that Fleming had been at Eton too.

When the sun shone, Lancelyn sat out on the terrace with his books and a drink. He took daily walks along the Croisette or the Rue d'Antibes and in the evening he relaxed in a hot tub or went to the Casino and gambled small sums of money. *The Times Crossword* arrived a day late. He did not bother with the rest of the newspaper. He avoided speaking to any of the other guests. He heard nothing from Bernard and fantasised that he must be staying with one of his imaginary aunts.

By the time Lancelyn returned to Oxford, his parents had moved on to Caracas.

They were idle rich and it was hard to imagine anyone idler or richer, though they complained to him of the most excruciating boredom. It was now Hilary Term and he gave up rowing in order to concentrate on work. He saw less of Bernard this term. It was part of Bernard's act that he never did a stroke of work, but this was indeed an act and, in order to keep it up, he had to seclude himself in small and obscure libraries where he hoped he would not be seen to be diligently reading and taking notes. The other reason Bernard seemed to be less about was because of his frequent visits to Somerville.

'You have got to come with me next time. The place has to be seen to be believed. They are supposed to be reading Classics, French or Forestry, but that seems to be all a lot of ballyhoooo. In reality Somerville is the Grand Seraglio of north Oxford. It is just like that painting by Ingres, *Le Bain Turc*. You know the one. There they are, all young women, sitting, standing and languorously lying about, just like in the painting – except that they have got their clothes on of course.'

'Ah.'

'And so, once through the door and past that dragon

of a doorkeeper, I find that wherever I turn, I see oodles of embonpoint on display and at the same time I become conscious of being observed by so many eyes, flashing eyes, doe eyes, smiling eyes, and behind all those eyes the light of love and the longing to be loved. Feminine *espièglerie*, is there any other kind? I fancied that I could hear their siren voices pleading for them, no, for us, to be allowed a bit of canoodling. I felt myself to be the Pasha of all I surveyed, for I could see that they were all *jeunes filles en fleur* and definitely up for some umpus bumpus.'

But Lancelyn was not tempted by this vision of the Grand Seraglio of north Oxford.

Towards the end of Hilary Term something extraordinary happened. He was coming back to his rooms after a tutorial with Nevill Coghill on the relationship between Shakespeare's plays and the revenge tragedies when Garner stopped him in the quad and warned him, 'Sir, there is a woman in your study. I thought it best to let her wait inside.'

A woman in his rooms! How strange. It could not be his mother. She was currently in Paris.

The woman was Molly Ransom. She had been sitting at his desk but with her back to it, and she now rose and made an apologetic gesture, 'Dear Mr Delderfield, may I call you Lancelyn? Bernard has talked so much about you that I feel that I know you already.'

Lancelyn nodded and gestured that she should resume her seat. He retreated to the dilapidated armchair in the corner of the room. There was a very long silence. Finally she spoke again, 'Actually it is about Bernard that I have come. I know that you are his friend, his good friend and he deserves his friends and… oh dear, this is awkward… you see I have come to ask you to use your influence to stop your friend visiting me in my college. I am afraid that he is nursing unrealistic hopes of some kind of emotional relationship. Those hopes are not reciprocated by me and besides the frequency of his visits and his ridiculous way of speaking are causing talk in the college. He doesn't seem to hear anything I say, but he might listen to you. You are my best hope.'

Lancelyn was silent and thinking frantically. Certainly, however this played out, it was going to be extremely awkward. Even more awkward than he had anticipated, for at the next moment she had risen and crossed the room to throw herself at his feet and place a hand on one of his legs. One thing Eton did not teach you was how to deal with girls.

'Please, you have to help me,' she said. 'I can never be his "popsy".'

How to get rid of the hand?

'Would you like a cigarette?'

She shook her head.

'Well, I would. I need to think how to go about this.'

She reluctantly removed her hand and got back on her feet and this allowed him to stride over to his desk and find his cigarette case. Meanwhile she wandered over to his bookshelves.

'What a lot of books!'

'I assure you that they are designed for use rather than ostentation.'

'Hmm.' She ran her fingers over some of them. 'They are awfully dusty. I could come here another time with a feather duster and clean them for you.'

'I rather think that my scout would be awfully put out to see me employing the most glamorous charlady in all of Oxfordshire,' he replied with awkward gallantry. 'Besides I prefer them dusty. Sherlock Holmes would never allow Mrs Hudson to dust his books, because he reckoned that the thickness of the dust on their respective tops gave him a good idea of when he had last consulted each of them. But come, if you have never been to Merton before, you must not leave before admiring our beautiful garden.'

He opened the window and stepped out onto the lawn before in turn helping her to step out from his room. At last he had his cigarette alight and he was thinking furiously. She was looking round in wonder. The walls of the parapet that separated the Fellows' Garden from Dead Man's Walk glowed yellow in the sunlight of late afternoon. A gleaming armillary sundial stood close to a rather frail-looking walnut tree that had been planted in the reign of James I. The sound of Chopin floated across the garden from the music room at the far end.

She gazed in wonder. Then, 'Sod it. Somerville has nothing like this.' She was bitter. Then, 'You don't want to do this, do you? Say something.'

He shook his head before reluctantly replying, 'Surely you are capable of telling him that he is wasting his time. Just tell him to push off.'

Then she smiled, but her smile was grim.

'He says that you are his best friend, but I wonder if you really know him. He may play the silly ass, but underneath he is completely ruthless. He will stop at nothing to get what he wants and what he wants is me. I am actually frightened of what he will do to me if I turn him down again and yet I am even more frightened of what he will do to me if I do not turn him down. But you must be strong enough to deal with him.'

(If only they had not gone for that drink at The Chequers last term.)

'Very well, I will see what I can do.'

At which point she lunged up at him and, knocking the cigarette out of his mouth, kissed him on the lips. Then at last he was able to escort her out of the college.

He did not find it easy to sleep that night. How on earth was he going to take this up with Bernard? And was Bernard really ruthless? Was he in truth like the Scarlet Pimpernel, affecting the manners of a foppish chinless wonder, but secretly masterminding coups and the elimination of all who opposed him? No, it was absurd. But it was inevitable that visions of Molly should mingle with his thoughts on that matter. He added her to his harem of phantom succubi and masturbated to her image. ('Masturbation' was 306.77.)

Molly was now queen of the harem. Was she not lovely? But, when he thought of all that hair, he thought of the M.R. James story 'Canon Alberic's Scrapbook' and the long coarse hair of the monstrous creature that sought to attack the scholar by night. But no, he dismissed this wholly inappropriate image. She was a woman and surely every woman 'that came his way was an immense world of delight closed to his senses five'. Women were lovely, kind and soft. But then, without wishing to, he found himself drifting on to recall the horrid climax of another story by the same author, 'The Treasure of Abbot Thomas', in which the thing, whatever it was, released from its dark hiding place by another over-curious scholar 'slipped forward on to my chest, and *put its arms around my neck*'. In this manner the investigator 'became acquainted with the extremity of terror and repulsion which a man can endure without losing his mind'. Lancelyn tried instead to think of Molly clinging to him and the consequent arousal of his desire, but almost immediately he found himself worrying once more about what to say to Bernard. And so things went round and round. Finally he resorted to reciting a couple of lines from Catullus:

> *'Odi et amo. Quare id faciam requiris*
> *Nescio, sed fieri et excrucior.'*

He did this again and again until finally towards dawn, lulled by the unholy mantra, he fell asleep.

It was a while before the opportunity to confront Bernard seemed to present itself. Neither of them often dined in hall, but two weeks later they found themselves sitting opposite each other at dinner. Bernard was talking loudly and madly about the gherkin, 'the uncrowned queen of all the vegetables', when Lancelyn cut in, 'Bernard I need to talk to you about a certain lady in Somerville –'

'A certain lady!' Bernard interrupted. 'Molly Ransom seems utterly uncertain as to –'

At which point Bernard was in his turn interrupted by the man sitting on his left, Henry Powys, a rather obnoxious scientist whom Lancelyn vaguely knew from rowing sessions.

'I challenge you to a sconce,' Powys said.

Talking about religion, politics or work during dinner in hall at Merton was banned. Drawing attention to the pictures in the hall fell under the ban and so was the mention of a lady's name. Anyone who broke that rule might be sconced which is to say obliged to drink a yard of ale, which was two and a half pints of beer, in a single draught and, if he failed, he had to pay for the beer. Bernard first exercised his right to appeal to the high table. This had to be done in a classical language, and so he scribbled a note in Latin to the effect that Molly Ransom was not a real woman, but only a character in a novel and hence a mere *flautus voci*. His appeal was rejected.

Though Lancelyn approved of ancient rituals, the timing of the invocation of this one was inconvenient. Bernard successfully downed his first yard of ale in one go and, since he had done so, his challenger had to attempt the same or pay for Bernard's beer. But he was also successful and so one of the waiters presented another tankard. Bernard hesitated, but then tipped the entire draught down his throat. The challenge went back to Powys who grimly managed his second yard. By now bets were surreptitiously being taken up and down the tables and all the waiters were standing round the pair. Bernard, presented with his third tankard downed it with a splashy flourish and smiled beerily at his opponent. At which point Powys surrendered and paid for all the beer. Lancelyn and Bernard had to leave their dinners unfinished as Bernard had to be supported out of the hall and across the quad. Lancelyn lugged him up the stairs and dumped him on his bed. So the opportunity had passed and Lancelyn found that he just could not muster the strength of will to broach the matter on any future occasion. Alas.

Three weeks later he was coming out of Thornton's second-hand bookshop when he found his way barred by Molly.

'Ah Mr Delderfield, I have got something for you.'

'I hope it is something nice.'

'Well, it will certainly suit you. You have not spoken to Bernard have you? What is it with you? Were you just too bloody idle to do the decent thing? Or is it that you are afraid of him? Perhaps you should be. He is tougher and cleverer than you… bloody hell, you are trembling right now. Are you even afraid of me as well? Why for fuck's sake could you not have talked to him?'

'Video meliora proboque deteriora sequor.'

'What the fuck is that supposed to mean?'

'"I see better things and approve; I follow the worse." It is Ovid from *The Metamorphoses*.'

'Is it now? Well across the fucking centuries you and Ovid are a pair of shits. And now here is your present.'

With that she fished into her handbag and produced a white feather which she stuck in the buttonhole of his suit and then she marched away down The Broad.

A white feather! So old-fashioned. That sort of thing became passé after the First World War. Now the honourable thing, the exciting thing, the redemptive thing would be for him to return to his rooms, pack a few things, travel down to London, enlist in the army, seek to be sent to fight in somewhere hot and dangerous like Sudan and finally come back to Oxford, a bemedalled hero and return the white feather to Molly. Then perhaps he might yet be the subject of her hypothetical novel. No, on reflection, he did not want to feature in anything that she might write, and besides going off to fight in Sudan would be more excitement than he felt that he could take. As for the white feather, it might do for a quill pen. But, alas no, it looked like a chicken feather and not strong enough to write with. He needed cheering up. He went back into the shop and bought an expensive facsimile edition of Francesco Colonna's *Hypnerotomachia Poliphili*. That night he dreamt of a black-haired woman, clad only in a shift, who climbed up a tree and cut off twigs with a curved knife.

She smiled at him and said, 'I thought that this tree needed a bit of pruning.' He thanked her and hurried on for he had a bus to catch, though he would almost certainly miss it. One of his typically boring dreams.

The rest of the term passed without incident. Then came Trinity Term which was full of preparations for exams, followed by the exams themselves. The last of the finals papers was on the third of June. There were a dozen English Literature finalists from Merton that year and three of them had invited their girlfriends to meet them at the end of the exams, and one of those three was Molly. She had been waiting for Bernard as he stepped out of the Examination Schools. Raven was also at the steps and he conducted his flock of finalists and the girls to the small lawn on Merton Street beside the Examination Schools. There the champagne was just being opened.

Champagne fell under technology, then, narrowing it down, home and management, then food and drink, then drinks, then wine. So it was 641.22. Lancelyn shook his head to clear it.

'Well that was a doddle,' said Bernard. 'It was like shooting fish in a barrel. I felt like answering all the questions on the paper instead of the requisite four.'

Having dismissed 641.22 from his mind, Lancelyn said nothing. He too had found the paper pretty easy and he had even managed to get references to Bram Stoker and Sheridan Le Fanu into a question about Victorian popular literature. Also, as with the earlier papers, he had found the sub fusc garb of the women candidates – white blouse, dark skirt, black stockings – pleasant to look upon on the occasions he paused for thought. Nevertheless, right now when he should have been exulting, he felt too unnerved by the unexpected appearance of Molly. How was this going to work out? The other ten candidates, who had not found this paper a breeze, scowled at Bernard. (They had more respect for Lancelyn because he had been a rowing man.) Bernard, no longer in coloured waistcoat and spats, but in the regulation sub fusc like the rest of them, suddenly looked rather ordinary.

Molly, who presumably had noticed how anxious Lancelyn was looking, came over with a glass of champagne for him.

'Lancelyn, let me kiss you.'

He was too startled to stop her. Other finalists looked on in envy. She continued, 'You did nothing and I bless you for that. You may be lazy or cowardly, but you are still a darling. Bernard says that what you did is follow what old India hands used to call a "policy of masterly inactivity". Don't look so surprised. You are quite forgiven. I don't know what I thought I was doing when I came to your rooms a couple of terms ago, but perhaps in some funny way I was testing myself and the strength of my feelings for Bernard and, perhaps without knowing it, you helped me pass that test.'

'After that white feather I thought of going away and joining the Foreign Legion,' Lancelyn said stupidly.

'I am so glad you didn't. You and Bernard should always

be together as friends, and now you must be my friend too. We have much to talk about.'

But as she stood there smiling, Lancelyn felt that, however Finals turned out, perhaps he had already failed to sit the only exam that mattered in life. Raven came up with a glass of champagne for Molly and now Lancelyn introduced them to each other.

After some conventional politenesses, Raven reverted to his unconventional self and addressing Lancelyn and Bernard, 'Now all that is over, you should put English literature behind you. In almost all ways a degree in English literature is a bad training for life. The novels you have been forced to read – *Tom Jones, Emma, David Copperfield, The Master of Ballantrae* – are linear. But the real world is not quite like that, for the construction of what is called "reality" relies on hidden symmetries, echoes and incidents that hint at other incidents and incidents that seem at first merely to be happenings will be found to be pointers to something real but yet unspeakable. A certain incident's ripples will spread out and the past will reconfigure itself as you leave it behind. Life is not a straight road… but enough. I must not talk shop. This is all behind you and you need never think about English literature again. Read only thrillers and science fiction if you need to read.'

'Actually I thought of working for a PhD in English Literature,' said Lancelyn.

(Though he could of course do nothing, he certainly did not want to follow his parents' example.)

'So am I,' said Bernard.

'Ah, the golden calf of research!' Raven groaned. 'And all my teaching gone for nothing. Research is a nasty, unnecessary thing which is ruining universities. It narrows the mind, cuts you off from other human beings and delays your entry into real life. Research prepares you for nothing except more research. Only second-raters go in for it. Only second-raters need their ghastly little diplomas. Worst of all, research teaches you to write like an academic.'

They had heard this rant of Raven's before.

'What will your thesis topic be?' Molly, turning to Lancelyn, wanted to know.

'I thought something on M.R. James and his *Ghost Stories of an Antiquary*,' replied Lancelyn.

He had been thinking for some months about researching the stories of M.R. James. What attracted him to them was that they belonged to an era that was past or soon to be so. Ghost stories, like printed collections of sermons or fables, had been produced for a readership that was no more. The genre belonged to an England that was firmly there only a few years ago, but no longer. The great age of the ghost story was passing, like London trams, circulating libraries, village blacksmiths and those AA men wearing peaked caps, gauntlets and riding jodhpurs who saluted passing drivers from their motorbikes. All gone or going. Come to that, the antiquary was on the way out too.

But, 'Snap, so was I,' said Bernard. We can't both work on the same thesis topic. One of us must back down. How do we decide?'

'I said it first.'

'So what?'

'How about arm-wrestling for a decision?' Lancelyn suggested.

'No, you are much stronger than I am. But how about the arbitration of chance? Here is a half crown. Will you stand by the toss of a coin?'

'I stand by it,' said Lancelyn. 'Heads, I get M.R. James. Tails, you do.'

The coin was spun and it fell tails. Goodbye to James then.

'The lot has been cast,' cried Bernard. 'Fate is with me!'

'I thought you did not want to stay in Oxford,' Lancelyn protested.

'Molly has still a year to go with her degree. I can start my research here. After that we will see.'

'Well, I won't supervise either of you,' and with that, Raven left them to go over and talk to the others. One of them (one of the other oiks as Lancelyn and Bernard called them, though not, of course, to their faces) a bit drunk already, had been denouncing Raven and his colleagues for not having taught them actually to enjoy Shakespeare or Dickens.

'After three years I still don't like them.'

'Oh really?' replied Raven. 'And if you had signed up for a chemistry degree, would you would expect to be taught how to delight in the smells of sulphur and ammonia? As it is, I have taught you to know the enemy and that is excellent. In years to come you should obviously steer clear of those authors.'

Other oiks were commenting on the failure of the generals' putsch in Algeria, and speculating about the prospects for the Evian talks and what was likely to happen next in France. None of this earnest stuff was of interest to Lancelyn and Bernard. But Molly had brought along a copy of *The Times* for Bernard who now shared it with Lancelyn, and sprawled out on the grass with their champagne, they fell upon the crossword. They took turns over the clues and Molly watched in wonder as they simultaneously rearranged anagrams in their heads. Bernard, who was as obsessed with the crossword as Lancelyn was, used to boast that he liked to solve it in the time it took to boil an egg. Lancelyn once timed it and found that it took Bernard twenty-four minutes, whereupon Bernard claimed that he liked his eggs very hardboiled. By now the oiks had drifted on to discussing Hugh Gaitskell's difficulties with the party he was supposed to be leading. Clearly bored with this, Raven came back to Lancelyn and Bernard and stood over them and watched for a while. Finally, 'So this is what a cryptic crossword looks like!'

(Had he really never seen a cryptic crossword before? Raven was amazing.)

'I now see that it is the whole world in little and a child's version of the world's mystery, so that it is something that can be played with,' he said and paused before continuing, 'Its clues are so many hidden messages. Johannes Trithemius, in his *Steganographia* of 1499, called this kind of thing "covered writing". He boasted that all the secrets of cryptoanalysis had been revealed to him in a dream.'

Was Raven or Trithemius drunk?

'Well I wish Trithemius was here now to give us a hand with the covered messages,' said Bernard. 'As it is, reason totters on its throne and it is all a bit of a strain on the grey matter.'

Raven was irritated by the interruption and continued, 'Trithemius tried to show us how secret messages could be conveyed by the planetary angels and how the messages' meanings might be revealed by them at the ends of their journeyings. If I understand the working of your crossword rightly, its clues seem to say one thing, but intend another, so that their meaning is simultaneously hidden and yet in plain sight. And so the crossword has emerged from a telepathic shadow world of the fifteenth century.'

Quite soon and without the recourse to telepathy the crossword was finished, and Raven wandered off again.

'God! If he can get all that out of a crossword, what will he make of a game of tiddlywinks?'

'That is easy,' replied Lancelyn. 'The upward flight of the game's plastic discs betokens the upward striving of minerals, plants, animals, men and angels in their ascent through the Great Chain of Being towards their union with the ineffable Oneness.'

'Er... what about the descending parabola of the tiddly-wink?'

'Manifestly, it betokens the dark descent of those fallen souls who have failed to eff the ineffable Oneness.'

'You make tiddlywinks sound quite challenging. We must have a game soon.'

Since the crossword had been finished and the champagne had run out, it was time to be going. Molly looked impatient. She had obviously been bored by the crossword and now she wanted Bernard for herself.

'We should know our results in exactly six weeks' time,' said Bernard. 'Let us meet up in London the day after the results are announced and, if necessary, drown our sorrows. Even if not necessary, let us drown our sorrows anyway.'

'Yes, let's. I suggest we meet at Le Macabre. There is

someone who may be there whom I would like you to meet. There is a good chance he will be there.'

'As long as it is not that Trithemius chappie. He sounded like a bit of a wanker. But otherwise fine. I will meet you at Le Macabre.'

Lancelyn gave Bernard the address. Then they went over to thank Raven for the champagne and, beyond that, the tuitions.

'Come and see me sometime. I shall miss you two.'

Walking away from the champagne lawn, Lancelyn found himself thinking about Molly. He was not sure why, but perhaps it was that he feared that she might destroy his friendship with Bernard. But could this happen? Nothing was certain except that things were changing and, when he would look back on this day in forty years' time, he would find that, all unaware, he had already been living in the past. His announcement just now (or rather then?) that he wanted to do research surprised no one more than himself. But it must be right for him to seek to avoid the fate of his parents who were driven from one part of the globe to another by the furies of boredom. After all life *per se* was boring. As someone (but who?) once remarked, 'People say that life is the thing, but I prefer reading.' And Lancelyn definitely preferred reading. But then, if research on James was now out of the question, then what or who to read about and research? So much was vague and uncertain.

By the time he reached his rooms so many questions and so much vagueness and uncertainty had led his thoughts to coalesce around one figure, Walter de la Mare, whose meditations in prose and poetry on the mysteries of existence and non-existence were paradigms of vagueness and uncertainty. De la Mare had been the master of stories that had no conclusion, stories full of twilight shadows, hints and things unspoken that left the reader wondering if he had quite understood what he was reading. Though de la Mare had once been grand and much honoured as a writer of the first rank and had died only a few years' back in 1956, he was already utterly out of fashion and practically forgotten. It would be Lancelyn's challenge to make him famous again and, more specifically, have his ghost stories recognised as clearly superior to those of M.R. James. But, of course, all this depended on him getting a decent degree.

Lancelyn spent the next three days in bed reading Robert Musil's *Der Mann ohne Eigenschaften*. Then it was time for him to move out of Merton and head for London. His parents had allowed him to make use of their flat in Albany while he decided what to do next. He enrolled in the London Library to begin reading de la Mare. He had put most of his books in store, an action that felt weirdly liberating, but within days of arriving in the city he felt compelled to start hunting for more books in the second-hand bookshops that clustered round the British Museum and lined Charing Cross Road and he experienced once more the thrill of the dusty chase. The bookshops served as repositories of rejected knowledge and in searching their shelves there was always the hope of coming across books that not only embodied rejected knowledge, but also knowledge that was rejected precisely because it was dangerous and forbidden. Then occasionally on sunny days, while waiting for the degree result, in order to clear his head, he went sculling up the Thames. He heard from Marcus that Bernard had been summoned by the examiners to a viva.

Presumably his degree was going to be a borderline something. Lancelyn received notification of his first at the beginning of August. His parents, who were then in Macao, were pleased and sent a congratulatory telegram.

CHAPTER THREE

To walk towards Le Macabre Coffee House in Meard Street was to step back into his past and to summon up his schoolboy excursions from Eton into Soho in his quest amidst its pubs, clubs and clip joints for really juicy pornographic magazines. Though it was now August, Lancelyn's walk brought back to him his blunderings in the smogs of past winters. During one such 'pea-souper' the smog briefly cleared and the boy that he was found himself staring at Le Macabre. He went in and no sooner had he sat down than Iron Foot Jack came and sat uninvited beside him. He introduced himself as a 'perfessor of physiolomy' and started to talk at length about the mysteries of existence and Caballer, as the Buddha, Swedenborg and Aleister Crowley had revealed them to him.

'I 'ave taken a fancy to you and I'm able to show you wonders,' he had concluded. 'I can show you how in your dreams you may yet 'ave eternal youth.'

From his first year at Eton onwards, there were many who had taken a fancy to Lancelyn, but now he said nothing. So Jack continued, 'I can see from the way you're looking at me that you are thinking 'ow someone as old as me and looking as I do, a poor old raspberry ripple, can offer anybody the dream of eternal youth. Oh yeah, I can read minds and I know exactly what you are thinking. So be careful what you think. Appearances are deceptive and a prince can appear in a totter's rags.'

(Months passed before Lancelyn discovered that 'raspberry ripple' was rhyming slang for 'cripple'. It was not be confused with 'raspberry tart' which was a 'fart'.)

But then the man who operated the espresso machine answered the phone on the counter and came to their table and tapped Jack on the shoulder.

'You are wanted over in Dean Street.'

'I 'ope they have got somewhere warm for us,' said Jack to him. Then turning to Lancelyn, 'I'm wanted. It's film work for me, a crowd scene. But I've taken a fancy to you and, if you summon me, no matter when and no matter what the circumstances, put out the word for me and I will come to you.'

Evidently cheered by the prospect of work, he stomped out of the coffee bar, singing as he went:

> Oh! it is really a werry pretty garden,
> And Chingford to the eastward could be seen;
> Wiv a ladder and some glasses,
> You could see to 'Ackney Marshes,
> If it wasn't for the 'ouses in between.

A few years had passed since Lancelyn had last visited Le Macabre and it felt like déjà vu to be walking once more down the narrow cobbled alley that ran between Dean and Wardour Streets. He feared that Le Macabre might have vanished, but there it was and he felt years fall away as he stepped inside and ordered a coffee before settling to the crossword. (Coffee was 641.3373 and coffee bars, if he remembered rightly, fell, under 647.95, eating and drinking places.) There was no sign of Jack. But Bernard arrived a few minutes later. He was without a waistcoat and instead he was wearing a black leather jacket. Was this his idea of slumming it? Bernard took in the frescoes of skeletons dancing with naked women, the coffins that served as tables and the ashtrays shaped like skulls. Though he looked most unhappy, it was not the décor that distressed him.

'I assumed that we would be meeting in a pub or a club, where one could get a drink, a proper drink that is,' he said. 'I have never been in a coffee bar before. Stone cold sober, a man could get the collywobbles in a reely 'orrible place like this.' He waved his arms. 'Woohoo!'

Then, having sat down and continuing to look around, 'So here it is at last, that distinguished thing. Do I really have to drink coffee? Well anyway, who was it that you wanted me to meet?'

'He is called Iron Foot Jack. I don't know his real name.'

'And is he here? What does he look like?'

'He has long dank black hair. When I met him he was wearing a broad-brimmed hat, a white frilled shirt and a black coat which stretched almost to his ankles – or rather to his ankle. And then there is his iron foot, of course.'

'The place is rather dark and crowded, but I can't see anyone with an iron foot, though it is difficult with so many coffins in the way. How come he has an iron foot? A most unusual prosthetic choice, I would have thought.'

'It's not exactly an iron foot, but rather a kind of metal frame attached to a surgical boot. The man at the bar told me that Jack told him that, while pearl fishing in the Coral Sea, he had lost his foot to a shark. Jack regularly sits in this place waiting for occasional work as a film extra. But he is not here. If he was, we would know by the smell. '

(Lancelyn had been hoping that an encounter with Jack might at least momentarily shock Bernard out of his posh silly ass act.)

'If the shark got his foot, what is in the boot?' Bernard asked. 'No, I suppose there are some things that mankind is not meant to know. Anyway, Molly will be along shortly. She is just doing some shopping. But how are you?'

'Very much as ever,' replied Lancelyn, 'which is to say, burning with a hard gem-like flame. And you?'

'Things are wonderful… sort of. Molly is quite wonderful. That said, living with a muse can be quite challenging, particularly if it is with the Muse of Swearing. She says that, since she finds herself in this world run by men, she finds that she can only operate as someone who will inspire a man. I am not sure that I quite believe all her muse stuff, but anyway, speaking as the man who is going to be thus inspired, it feels more like a threat than a promise. You know the story of Thamyris?… Thamyris challenged the muses to compete with him in singing and poetry. If he won, he got to sleep with all nine of them. But he did not win and they smashed his lyre in

42

front of his eyes, before cutting those eyes out.'

No sooner had Bernard finished speaking than Molly walked in, laden with shopping. The volume of noise in the café dropped slightly as men turned briefly to look at her. Well, she was beautiful enough to be a muse, but Lancelyn had expected that it would be just him and Bernard meeting today. Now her presence might put a crimp on their conversation. And besides he could not be sure that she really had forgiven him. But he greeted Molly ceremoniously and went to the counter to get her a coffee and ask after Jack.

The man at the counter shook his head, 'You have just missed him – by a couple of years. He died in hospital. Cancer took him a year or two ago.' He paused. 'But his smell lingers on.'

Lancelyn signalled to Bernard, wanting to know if he would like a coffee too, but he signalled back his disgust at the idea. When Lancelyn was seated again, he had to ask Bernard the question, 'I heard that the examiners called you in. Well?'

Bernard looked embarrassed and Molly replied for him, 'They just wanted to meet him, shake his hand and tell him that he had been awarded a First Class Degree, *summa cum laude*. And you?' she asked.

'Oh, just a middle of the road first-class honours.'

Bernard laughed, 'I'm sure it won't count against you in the long run.'

'The Dead March from Saul' had been playing on the jukebox, but since it had now finished, Molly went over to it and selected the *Liebstod* from *Tristan and Isolde*.

'That's much livelier,' said Bernard. 'One could dance to this one.'

A small group of young men and women who were sitting closer to the jukebox looked annoyed.

'So what will you do now?'

Again Bernard looked embarrassed, 'I am going to be sitting another exam, dammit. It's the All Souls Prize Fellowship examination. There will be an essay, a general paper and an essay on English literature. But I don't know…'

'It is only a formality,' Molly interrupted. 'He has already been told that the fellows really want him. But your weird guru Raven does not want him to get it because all they do in All Souls is research.'

'He may never speak to me again,' sighed Bernard.

Lancelyn felt really pleased for him… but envious too. Yes, of course, for he would not be human if he did not feel envy. Indeed there were times when he thought that he occasionally needed reassurance of this sort in order to prove to himself that he was human. He asked after Bernard's proposed research on M.R. James (hoping that, now this fellowship was in sight, he might have given up on the topic). But Bernard replied, 'I think that I have my title. I have read that Monty used to be in tears of laughter as he read P.G. Wodehouse to the boys at Eton. He loved Wodehouse and I think that there may be structural plot affinities between James and Wodehouse. Anyway I have my title, *The Full Monty: The Ghost Stories of an Antiquary Considered as a Comedic Masterpiece*. One would indeed have to be a dead and stuffed fish to read his ghost stories without roaring with laughter.'

'You are being fucking ridiculous,' said Molly.

The *Liebstod* had finished and Lancelyn was about to get up and put another record on, when one of the young men at the table by the jukebox went over to the counter to complain about its noise. So the man at the counter went over to pull the plug on it. Without the music, the conversation of the young men and their girlfriends could be clearly heard. They were talking about the need to let it all hang out, generate only good vibes, eventually hit the road and so find dharma, stuff like that. Their uniform of roll-necked black pullovers proclaimed that they were beatniks. They were now joined by another long-hair who was in a strange-looking coat and their conversation grew louder.

This is the shape of the future, thought Lancelyn, hairy, dirty, pretentious and noisy. Now it came to him that he had read about this weird coat with hood and toggle fastenings. It was called a duffel coat. Though the twentieth century had started slowly, every day there seemed to be more and more small signs of its gathering pace. He decided that he did not care for the duffel coat.

'Are you not going to write down their conversation?' he asked Molly.

She looked embarrassed, 'I have given that up. It was all bollocks about becoming a novelist. I haven't written a fucking word. Instead I think I may become Bernard's muse and, what's more, I am going to modernise him. All Souls might be a stepping stone to other things. Maybe politics.'

What extraordinary things to come out with! But, though there had been no such thing as a Muse of Learned Dissertations on Mount Parnassus, perhaps there should have been. Then, how exactly did a woman go about becoming a muse? He was about to ask her, when Bernard slammed his fist on the table and shouted, 'What the deuce! Can't a fellow enjoy scary music anymore? That can easily be remedied.'

And with that he stood to sing at the top of his voice:

'When the night wind howls in the chimney cowls, and
the bat in the moonlight flies,
And inky clouds, like funeral shrouds, sail over the
midnight skies –
When the footpads quail at the night-bird's wail,
And black dogs bay at the moon,
Then is the spectres' holiday – then is the ghost's high
noon!
High nooooon!'

Molly looked even more uncomfortable and one of the beatniks
made a deprecating gesture, 'Hey, cool it. Okay, man?'

But Bernard continued singing and now Lancelyn stood
to join in:

'As the sob of the breeze sweeps over the trees, and the
mists lie low on the fen,
From grey tomb – stones are gathered the bones that
once were women and men,
And away they go with a –'

At this point they were ordered to leave. Out in the street they
linked arms with a reluctant Molly and continued singing
W.S. Gilbert's 'The Ghosts' High Noon'. In between verses,
Bernard shouted, 'I need a proper drink.'

They only stopped singing when they entered The French
Pub. Lancelyn and Molly shared a bottle of wine. Bernard

46

ordered a Dog's Nose, which proved to be a mixture of gin and bitter ale, and the second dose of this concoction had the merciful effect of calming him down. Lancelyn was asked about his proposed research.

'Since Raven has refused to take me on, someone called Magree at Worcester is going to supervise me. I thought that I might do something on Walter de la Mare.'

'Good move. No one reads him anymore, so you will be able to get away with saying practically anything. A bit dull though.'

Yes, why could de la Mare not have taken drugs, slept with a hermaphrodite dwarf, kept a pet wombat, sold guns in Abyssinia and committed suicide in prison? As it was, he wrote poetry in a jacket and tie. But what Lancelyn said was, 'I thought that I would work on the contrast between the sedate world he actually lived in and the faery world spun by his dreams. Yet it was precisely in this faery land that he was able to conjure up the beauty of horror.'

'Ah, he sounds perfect material for the old fart school of literary criticism.'

'So does your approach to M.R. James.'

Then Bernard and Lancelyn started to worry that there was a danger that they were about to become desiccated academics. They were throwing their lives away before life had really started and they needed another drink to deal with this. Then Bernard was grumbling about how he was going to have to find someone else to put him in a novel if Molly was not going to do it. Lancelyn offered to write about him for *The Reader's Digest* in its 'The Most Memorable Character I Ever Met' series. Then Molly was going on about how the three of them were going to be part of the country's future, but Lancelyn was thinking that was what women did. Driven by the life-force, they used their beauty to lure men into the future. Goethe had been the first to spot this. *Das Ewige-Weibliche zieht uns hinan.* The eternal in woman draws us on.

Having run out of ready money, they left The French Pub. They were too drunk to say goodbye properly.

'I am pissed as a parrot' declared Bernard. 'But we are young and thank God there are older and wiser men looking after our country.'

Lancelyn took an erratic course through Soho towards Piccadilly, past so many Italian and Greek delicatessens and other small shops, pawnbrokers, coffee bars and tattooing parlours in the dusty colours of summer. He passed sandwich-board men, musicians and lonely drunks who hunted for pleasure – or for women which would be almost as good. This too shall pass.

There had been something weird about their meeting, something missing or a sense of constraint. Then Lancelyn realised what it was. Not the black leather jacket, or not just the black leather jacket, but Bernard was almost talking like a normal person – not quite, but it was a close approximation.

Back in Oxford, he found a small flat to rent just beyond Folly Bridge. Raven, true to his word had refused to supervise his thesis on 'The Supernatural World in the Stories and Poems of Walter de la Mare'. So Lancelyn was referred to a specialist in poetry of the Georgian school, Professor Magree in Worcester. When, three weeks into the Oxford year, Lancelyn arrived for his second thesis supervision, things took an unexpected turn.

'I understand you have changed your thesis topic,' said Magree.

'No, I haven't.'

'Yes, you have,' Magree was emphatic. 'Edward Raven came to see me yesterday and he was good enough to inform me that there has been a misunderstanding and what you are actually researching is something on Sir Thomas Browne.'

'No, I am not. I don't understand.'

'That, I think, is perfectly understandable. I cannot think how I got the idea that you were working on de la Mare. Such a pity. It would have been rather a good thesis topic. As it is, the abrupt change of subject is somewhat irregular and the paperwork of the registration will need sorting out. Raven also asked me to pass this on to you.'

Magree handed to Lancelyn a cutting from *The Daily Telegraph*. The University of St Andrews English Department was looking to appoint a lecturer and preference would be given to a suitable candidate who was a specialist in seventeenth-century literature. Magree allowed Lancelyn time to take this in before continuing, 'I will be one of your referees and Raven will be the other, but in order for us to write the supporting letters we will need to know the title of your thesis and also see an outline sketch of its planned contents. If you could let us both have copies of this necessary information by this time next week, we shall be able to write what is necessary. You should put your application in as fast as possible, naming us as your referees. And now I do not think that we need bother with Walter de la Mare today. Good luck!'

Lancelyn did what he was told and back at the flat he took Browne's *Pseudodoxia Epidemica* down from his shelves.

Browne's treatise, spread over three volumes, came to over seven hundred pages and it took him a day and a half to get through. Then he fetched out Robert Burton's *The Anatomy of Melancholy*, which weighed in at over a thousand pages and got through that too in a day and a half. Then he composed a two-page synopsis of his marvellous new thesis, *Taxonomies of Error and Madness in the Works of Sir Thomas Browne and Robert Burton*, and he sent off copies of this to St Andrews, Raven and Magree. Perhaps de la Mare was not going to become famous again after all.

Though Bernard was also back in Oxford, they were respectively preoccupied with their forthcoming ordeals. Ever since schooldays Lancelyn's mind and therefore his world had been taxonomically ordered and numbered by him: first general methods, followed in order by philosophy and psychology, religion, social sciences, language, natural sciences and mathematics, technology, the arts, literature and rhetoric, history, biography and geography. He knew large parts of the Dewey Decimal System of library classification by heart. For example, take 100, which was the broad philosophy and psychology grouping. Within it was situated the much less broad subgroup 130, parapsychology and occultism, and this included 131, parapsychological and occult methods for achieving well-being happiness and success, 132, mental derangements, 133, specific topics in parapsychology and occultism, 134, mesmerism, 135, dreams and mysteries, 136, mental characteristics, 137, divinatory graphology, 138, physiognomy and, 139, phrenology. This was all in his head.

But this was nothing. He could instantly read the Dewey Decimal numerals as if they had been written out in plain

English. For example, take 371.97927567017521. 371.97, meant education. 927, was Arab and Maltese. 567, signified that the region in question was more specifically Iraq. The following zero functioned as a kind of full stop. 175, referred to regions where specific languages predominate and finally 21, referred to English. So, taken as a whole, the number string designated the education of Iraqi students in English-speaking countries. This was child's play to Lancelyn. Indeed he had mastered it as a child and it was his superpower. Moreover, the whole thing had been internalised, so that his own brain was decimally organised. But now his task was to demonstrate how in the seventeenth century Browne and Burton with their primitive hierarchies of classification were groping towards something like the Dewey Decimal System and nevertheless failing to do so.

He went up to St Andrews by train, leaving the sleeper at Edinburgh and changing on to the Leuchars line. The interview was in the afternoon. So he had plenty of time to walk right round the town. There were just three main streets and the place was like Toytown. It had a fire station, a police station, a church, a cinema, a grocer, a butcher, a toyshop and a public library – oh, and a ruined cathedral which Toytown did not have. What would it be like to be immured here, a kind of Ultima Thule, albeit one with a grocer and butcher? What would it be like to die here by the sea?

There were five people on the interviewing panel: the Professor and a Senior Lecturer from the English department, someone from the French department, the Head of the Arts Faculty and the Quaestor of the University. Lancelyn's Eton-bred confidence stood him in good stead in the interview.

Moreover, his immersion in Browne and Burton was still so recent that he had not yet had time to get bored with his supposed thesis topic and so he was able to speak with enthusiasm about all the research that he had been doing and that enthusiasm was all the greater for not having read any of the tedious critical literature on the subject. He spoke glibly about how in the seventeenth century Francis Bacon had developed a taxonomic structure whose hierarchy of knowledge was based on the medieval quadrivium and trivium, but later in the seventeenth century the natural sciences had led the western world in the development of a coherent and comprehensive taxonomy and in so doing managed to dispense with the Baconian hierarchies of relative importance.

The Professor, who worked on Victorian children's literature, and the Senior English Lecturer, who had published on Joseph Conrad, looked utterly bemused.

Towards the end of the interview, they got on to the subject of Shakespeare and *Hamlet*. Lancelyn was able to quote from Browne's *Religio Medici*: 'those apparitions and ghosts of departed persons are not the wandering souls of men, but the unquiet walks of Devils, prompting and suggesting unto mischief, blood and villainy'. This was the common view among learned folk of the age and it followed that the apparition of Hamlet's father at the start of the play was in fact that of a lying demon and therefore that the revenge Hamlet plotted was based on a satanic delusion. The Professor looked doubtful.

But, 'You will be hearing from us shortly.'

And he heard three days later that he had got the job.

CHAPTER FOUR

He arrived back in St Andrews four weeks before the beginning of the Candlemas term. It was midwinter and the haar, a dismally cold sea fret, drifted down the bleached grey streets and made the way uncertain. The sun, when one could see it, began to set soon after lunch. Why was he not in Trinidad sipping daiquiris with his parents? He lodged briefly in the Cross Keys Hotel, but lost little time in buying a grand house in Hepburn Gardens and engaging the services of a housekeeper.

The first departmental meeting convened a week before the beginning of term. He soon discovered that most of the staff in the department were Cambridge graduates and, that being so, there was embittered feuding between partisans of F.R. Leavis and those of C.S. Lewis. The Department of English was very English indeed and Lancelyn was introduced to just one lecturer who worked on a Scottish writer called

James Hogg, who was also known as 'the Ettrick Shepherd'. What did one have to do to become 'ettrick', Lancelyn wondered? Since Lancelyn was an Oxford graduate he was looked on as a curiosity, but both sides hoped to recruit him in the great feud. Moreover the Head of Department, who had difficulty in remembering his name, took to calling him 'Mr Oxford'. Lancelyn tried to reciprocate by not remembering the Professor's name, but it was Wormsley. There were no women in the department.

After welcoming the new member of staff, the departmental meeting got down to the agenda that had been laid out in advance: management of the departmental library, proposed improvements to the bicycle shed, the overuse of the cyclostyle machine and suchlike matters. The last item on the agenda was the most contentious and presumably it had been placed last in the doomed hope that it would not actually be reached. Now members of the Leavisite faction moved that most novelists should be removed from the syllabus, since they were not part of 'The Great Tradition'. The only novels that needed to be taught were those by Jane Austen, George Eliot, Henry James, Joseph Conrad and D.H. Lawrence. The rest were just fictions on which housemaids and ill-educated layabouts wasted unprofitable hours. The leader of the Lewis faction puffed furiously at his pipe, as did the Professor on his. Lancelyn was more relaxed with his Black Russians. It seemed a bit confusing at first but he soon worked out that the Leavisites did not wear ties.

Though the Leavisites looked intensely earnest about their mission of expurgation, the Lewisites sought to outmanoeuvre them by arguing that the Leavisite shortlist consisted of too much easy reading and that the students had to be stretched by being forced to read really difficult novels from the seventeenth and eighteenth centuries. Moreover, the specialist on Hogg thought it would be a bit odd if a literature department in a Scottish university did not allow space on its syllabus for such writers as Robert Louis Stevenson and George MacDonald. One of the younger Lewisites claimed that he had heard that housemaids and idlers were reading *Lady Chatterley's Lover* and he mischievously went on to suggest shortening the syllabus still further by also removing Lawrence from it. This caused so much outrage that Wormsley swiftly brought the debate to a close, called for a vote and then, claiming that the time was not ripe for such sweeping reform, he used his casting vote in favour of the status quo. Since neither Sir Thomas Browne nor Robert Burton had got round to writing a novel, Lancelyn had known himself to be a relaxed spectator in this argument and he had abstained. But it was certainly more interesting than the problems of the cyclostyle machine. In future departmental meetings he would take care to have *The Times Crossword* with him. So this was work! This was real life! Though he did not much care for it, it was manageable.

Lancelyn was replacing a previous lecturer who had died suddenly in obscure circumstances. So, for the term that was about to start, Lancelyn found himself committed to two lectures a week, as well as three first-year tutorial groups, and two second-year tutorial groups and it was four whole weeks before his lectures started. Whatever it was that his predecessor had died of, it was not overwork. So he mugged up a lot of bog-standard stuff on Francis Bacon, Bunyan, Lancelot Andrews, Milton, Donne, Herrick. Whatever did not come from his Oxford revision notes, mostly came from the Encyclopaedia Britannica.

Then dinner with Professor Wormsley was also part of the ritual induction to academic life in St Andrews – something which ought to have been part of the job description. On arrival he was carefully introduced to all the dinner guests and what happened was what always happened when he was carefully introduced to a string of people. All their names were immediately deleted from his memory. It was certainly inconvenient and it meant that he spent the entire evening in a social fog. He remembered the Professor of course – and his name, dammit. And the big woman who bustled about and gave orders to the servants was presumably the Professor's wife. He also recognised one of the lecturers who had been at the departmental meeting. It was the one who specialised in the 'Ettrick Shepherd'. During the dinner, one thing got clarified. He asked this man, whatever his name was, how one became ettrick. It turned out that Ettrick was a Lowland Scotland village. Lancelyn had been fantasising that the adjective was a Scots term for a primitive form of electricity. There was one rather beautiful young blonde at the table. When she spoke, her fluttery voice somehow suggested feathers. Too bad that he had not been able to hang on to her name. Apart from her, the other half-dozen guests were older men and women. They might have been academics. They might not have been. So he had to proceed cautiously as he spoke.

At first there was a lot of talk at table about town and gown in St Andrews and advice about where to shop – which, considering how few shops there were, was a bit superfluous. Then Lancelyn caused some embarrassment by asking

Wormsley how the university classified its books. Did it use the Dewey Decimal Library System, or was it some more idiosyncratic arrangement? Wormsley had no idea and neither had anyone else at the table. But how could anyone go into a library and not take interest in its classification system?

Lancelyn was going to say more, but he could see that everyone was looking at him oddly, so he stopped.

Only in retrospect did he realise what excitement his appearance at the dinner must have given rise to. Here was the most junior of lecturers who had started off by straightaway buying a mansion in Hepburn Gardens, in the same row in which the Provost and a handful of the most senior professors lived. So Lancelyn was seen as a Count of Monte Cristo figure. Where did his money come from? Gambling? A secret second life as a bestselling author? Buried treasure? Or he might be the illegitimate son of a senior politician? And soon there was to be much speculation about him in the town at large, where he was widely thought to be a young don who specialised in taxidermy. But those at the dinner table also wanted to know about Edward Raven, who, no less than Lancelyn, was a man of mystery, for Raven had never published anything, rarely lectured and was not known to have any special subject and yet he kept producing brilliant finalists.

Lancelyn's fellow diners could not ask him directly where his money came from. So they attempted all sorts of indirect questions. From what part of the country was he from? Were either or both his parents academics? Had he been abroad much? It was a bit like that game, Animal, Vegetable or Mineral, and Lancelyn, who was enjoying this game, tried as much as possible to confine his answers to 'yes' or 'no'. He played a similarly straight bat when it came to the supposed miraculous powers of Mr Raven and merely referred vaguely to his tutor's erudition and diligence. When Lancelyn could, he steered the conversation back to interesting walks around St Andrews.

Towards the end of the meal, the Professor's wife made a discreet signal to the other ladies and they withdrew to another room. It was now time for Wormsley to bring forth the port and whisky and, having done so, he began to talk about railway timetables. Lancelyn could see from the faces of the other four men that this was a favourite topic of the Professor. Although Wormsley did not seem to do that much travelling by train himself, he could still tell you the best way of travelling by rail from Dundee to Exeter while avoiding both Darlington and Crewe and, what is more, he could tell you the precise times of the necessary interchanges. The network of Britain's railways and their interlocking schedules were all held within his head. It was a marvel, if a somewhat boring one, and Lancelyn listened with a polite smile on his face.

But suddenly Wormsley swivelled round, 'I am boring you, aren't I, Mr Oxford?'

Lancelyn shook his head.

'Oh yes, I am! I know when I am being boring and I am not the complete fool that you take me for – or, indeed all of us for. Although you may not have found my discourse on the railways at all interesting, and normal people are usually bored by talk of timetables, I hope that you will admit, that, for your part, you have contributed singularly little to this evening's talk at table. You are not just bored with railway timetables. You are bored with all of us. I guess that you think that because we are provincials we are not up to your level.'

Lancelyn tried to say something at this point, but Wormsley silenced him with a gesture.

'I am not the fool that I look.'

He did indeed look a bit of a fool, with those bizarrely protruding eyebrows, bulging red cheeks and hairs seeming to stream out of his nostrils, but Lancelyn was not allowed to deny that striking resemblance, as Wormsley continued, 'I would have you know that I was not taken in by your performance at the interview and all that blarney about Sir Thomas Browne and his hitherto neglected ideas on taxonomy. Frankly I did not want you in my department, but I was outvoted by the others. Perhaps they thought that the students would be charmed by your handsome face and agreeable sounding voice and so they would be lured into doing third-year Eng. Lit. That may be right. But you have come here full of arrogance and expectations. I dare say you envisage your lectureship here in the sticks as a mere stepping-stone to something more respectable in Oxford or Cambridge. Well, I had better warn you, that unless you get your preposterous sounding doctorate done, you won't even get tenure here and that will be the end of any academic ambitions that you may have entertained. And, personally I don't care where all your bloody money comes from. I don't even want to know.'

Now at last Lancelyn was allowed to speak, 'I am sorry to have disappointed you. I had not realised that I was due to undergo a second vetting this evening.'

'I hope we now understand one another. From now on, Lancelyn, you may call me Edgar. Oh, and when Sheila, returns do try and make some kind of conversation with her.'

The others had sat over their drinks and listened with poker faces. Lancelyn only detected a hint of sympathy in the face of the young man who was an expert on things Ettrick. Now one of the others broke in with a question to Wormsley about the frequency of trains between Leuchars and Edinburgh and conversation limped along until the Professor's wife (who Lancelyn had belatedly gathered was called Sheila) returned with the other ladies and coffee was served. Wormsley was clearly a man for surprises and, as Lancelyn was standing at the front door saying his goodbyes and thanks, the Professor suddenly said, 'Now you are here, we must find you a mistress, possibly even a wife.'

That night Lancelyn introduced the young woman with the long blonde hair to his harem of phantom succubi. The following day Lancelyn visited the University Library which was housed in the Old Divinity School and was dismayed to discover that its books were not arranged according to the Dewey Decimal System, for the chief librarian had instead taken it into his head to adopt a system that was modelled on that of the US Library of Congress. So what might have been a well-ordered stroll through a neatly laid-out garden instead turned into a panicky exploration of a dark literary maze in which Lancelyn became completely lost amidst the dark and irregular corridors of shelving. Where did all this knowledge start and where did it end? *'Secretum meum mihi et filiis domus mihi.'* A man might die without finding what he wanted in such an ill-ordered accumulation of books. It was as if Lancelyn had been hit by a bullet of kryptonite and his superpower had become now useless. Only a visit to the little public library close by Holy Trinity Church and organised according to the

Dewey Decimal System helped restore his spirits a little bit.

He was living like a monk in St Andrews. He did miss Bernard, for together they had constituted a kind of Mr Bones-Mr Jones act in which they had taken turns in the roles of the comic and the straight man. But apart from missing Bernard, he would not be lonely, for he had his books. Once the carpenter had come to Hepburn Gardens to fit the necessary bookcases, it was time to summon the books out of store and get them back on shelves where he could see them. But the books were like surly dogs, who in their master's absence, had been confined in the kennels too long and were therefore at first reluctant to communicate with him. They demanded not just his attention, but also his contrition. Only slowly did they begin to speak to him as they had been accustomed to do and, then thanks to their companionship he found that he was not lonely, just bored.

Even so, he experienced the boredom as a tranquil and soothing thing, for though it was now 1962, St Andrews mostly rested in the early 1950s – such a time of innocence compared to the decade that was now happening in London and elsewhere. People up here had read about the Profumo Affair in the pages of *The Scotsman* and marvelled at it, as if it was something exotic happening on a distant continent. In the streets of St Andrews people greeted one another with a careful ceremoniousness. Groceries were wrapped in brown paper parcels and delivered to one's front door. One bought one's fish directly from the fishing boats in the little harbour. There were no traffic lights anywhere in the town. Few people had television sets and there was no coffee bar. The monthly excitement would be the church jumble sale. He delighted that the place was behind the times, since it was the future he dreaded.

The University of St Andrews had been busy shedding medicine and other science subjects to its sister University of Dundee across the Tay. Lancelyn, who hated science, was glad to see these subjects go. Science was responsible for manufacturing the future and, in so doing, ruthlessly making one generation after the next obsolete. That was what science was for. Already the world he had grown up in was under threat, since science had invented nuclear power, plastics, television and instant coffee. Doubtless the boffins would follow all this up with other horrid things. Then there was an appalling novelist called C.P. Snow who was insisting that everyone had to know what the Second Law of Thermodynamics was. Why?

He had briefly toyed with the idea of taking up golf, but then he remembered that someone had once described the game as 'the antechamber to death', and so he decided instead to buy a motorcycle, a BMW R60, which he then learnt to ride on a deserted airfield. He envied those people who described their dreams of flying. He had never had such dreams, but speeding away on his bike and swooping round corners with the wind shrieking, he imagined that this must be what a dream of flying would be like. Also he loved armouring himself in helmet, boots, gloves and full leathers. He loved the look, the smell, the noise and, above all, the speed of his motorbike, though its workings were a complete mystery to him. The cylinders, the tappets, the plugs – all that belonged to the magical but sinister realm of science. The bike responded so swiftly to his impulses that it felt as much part of his body as were his arms and legs and, if he were to die, he thought that he would have his bike buried with him. He raced off on it along Scotland's empty roads to what were invariably scruffy and disordered second-hand bookshops in Dundee, Perth, Cupar and elsewhere on a hunt for first editions of Stevenson. When, dressed from head to foot in black and carrying his helmet he walked into a shop, the bookseller would almost always start with fear, faced with what he imagined might be an armed raider or some kind of special-forces policeman. Then the bookseller would face another shock as Lancelyn would list the rare volumes he was looking for.

He wished that he dreamt of flying or of racing about on his motorbike, but his dreams were always so bloody dull and incoherent. 'Half our days we spend in the shadow of the earth, and the brother of death exacteth a third part of our lives,' according to Browne. 'But the phantasms of sleep do commonly walk in the great road of natural and animal dreams, wherein the thoughts or actions of the day are echoed and acted over in the night.' That was it. Surely Browne was pointing to the banality of dreams which relied on ill-digested scraps borrowed from waking life. Raven had compared dream narratives to those of professional novelists and poets and had pointed out the obvious, that the comparison was entirely in favour of the professionals. Dreams wanted to tell stories, oh yes, but they did not know how to do it properly and they kept losing the plot. Certain themes were repeated excessively. Just occasionally they got a decent narrative going, but then failed to provide any kind of climax and instead drifted on to quite a different story. Night after night they amateurishly tried for a memorable tale, but they always botched it. What did dreams dream of? Why publication of course! First, they hoped to be repeated by their recipients, once that sleep-stunned captive audience woke up, but, beyond that, the dreams hoped to make it into print. Some hope! The best dreams that had made it into print were those entirely fake dream narratives that had been carefully crafted by professional writers. Coleridge's 'Kubla Khan' was a case in point. Or take 'Last night I dreamt I went to Manderley again. It seemed to me I stood by the iron gate leading to the drive, and for a while I could not enter, for the way was barred to me.' The opening sentences of Daphne du Maurier's *Rebecca* had a fine prose rhythm which ordinary dreams could only dream of.

Lancelyn's most common dream was of looking for a lavatory or somewhere else to piss, whereas the German poet Novalis had proclaimed: 'Our life is no dream, but it should and will perhaps become one.' Sod that! Dreams were 135 in the Dewey Decimal System and that was uncomfortably close to 132, mental derangements. Since Lancelyn agreed with Raven on the awfulness of these things, he preferred to invent his dreams and then palm them off on other people as if he had really dreamt them, while ditching the tedious and incoherent stuff that he had actually been subjected to in the night. People were invariably impressed by the interesting 'dreams' that he was able to tell them about.

Then there were the first tutorials. St Andrews was thought to be a safe and sheltered place to send the young. Though Lancelyn was not yet ready at this very early stage to introduce any of his students to the Ignatian technique, in all other respects he sought to imitate Raven and his other Oxford tutors. As he did so, he wondered if, sometime decades earlier, Raven had learned to model his tutorials on those of yet an earlier teacher who in turn had modelled his tutorials on the ones he had received as a student, and so perhaps there might be a form of scholarly transmission that stretched all the way back to William of Ockham and Duns Scotus and so it was that medieval disputations continued to be held in 1960s St Andrews. Lancelyn for his part cared far more for what he taught than for the people he taught it to. The students were vessels for the transmission of ancient techniques of learning. In his tutorials the students would at first struggle desperately to agree with what they thought he was thinking, while he was cheerfully determined to disagree with anything they might argue, even if it had indeed been what he was thinking. Half way through the first term a Glaswegian youth, bolder than the rest had protested, 'At the beginning of the year you give us this enormous reading list of critical literature and then you spend all your tutorials and lectures telling us what bollocks all this critical literature is.' After the introductory first term, this, the second term of the first year, was devoted to medieval literature and so he found himself teaching *Sir Gawain and the Green Knight* and *Piers Plowman* and he and his tutorial groups were then in the strange business of imposing modern logic on medieval fantasies.

When Raven had heard of Lancelyn's appointment he sent him a short note felicitating him on the fact that, now he had an academic job, he no longer needed to do any research. Not doing any research might be fine in Oxford, but here in St Andrews Lancelyn was under threat from Wormsley. Besides Lancelyn actually wanted to do research and, after dashing off some outline notes for lectures on seventeenth-century literature, he decided that there would be nothing for it but to use the Ignatian technique to immerse himself in the works of Sir Thomas Browne. And yet something held him back, some presentiment that things might not work out so well with Browne.

CHAPTER FIVE

Though, four years back, the Oxford first-year study of English literature had been pretty conventional, and made even duller than it need have been by the vast amount of Anglo-Saxon they had to master, things had changed abruptly at the end of that year. Raven took a group of five favoured students to a reading week that was held in a Swiss chalet. Lancelyn and Bernard had been the only two first-year students among the five chosen by Raven. The week proceeded strangely. After dinner on the first evening and over plentiful glasses of gluhwein, Raven gave a reading. It was from the sixteenth-century *Spiritual Exercises* of St Ignatius of Loyola, and it was one of the Jesuit's prescribed exercises for the first week of spiritual training and it was on Hell:

The first point will be to see with the eyes of the imagination those great fires, and the souls as it were in the bodies of fire.

The second, to hear with the ears the wailings, the groans, the cries, the blasphemies against Christ our Lord, and against all his saints.

The third, to smell with the sense of smell the smoke, the brimstone, the filth, and the corruption.

The fourth, to taste with the taste of bitter things, such as tears, sadness, and the worm of conscience.

The fifth, to feel with the sense of touch how those fires touch and burn souls.

Making a colloquy with Christ our lord, to bring to memory the souls that are in hell.

Raven read this through twice before leading the conversation on to quite other matters. Lancelyn and Bernard presumed and feared that this was the beginning of a fraught Alpine week during which Raven would seek to draw them all to Christ and personal salvation. This was not so – or not exactly so. The following morning Raven spoke to them briefly about Charles Dickens, his literary career and his concerns for social issues before reading to them the first chapter of *Bleak House*. This began:

London. Michaelmas term lately over, and the Lord Chancellor sitting in Lincoln's Inn Hall. Implacable November weather. As much mud in the streets, as if the waters had but newly retired from the face of the earth, and it would not be so wonderful to meet a Megalosaurus, forty feet long or so, waddling like an elephantine lizard up Holborn Hill. Smoke lowering down from the chimney pots, making a soft black drizzle with flakes in it as big as full-blown snowflakes – gone into mourning, one might imagine, for the death of the sun. Dogs, undistinguishable in mire. Horses, scarcely better; splashed to their very blinkers. Foot-passengers, jostling one another's umbrellas, in a general infection of ill temper, and losing their foot-hold at street-corners, where tens of thousands of other foot passengers have been slipping and sliding since the day broke (if this day ever broke), adding new deposits to the crust upon crust of mud, sticking at those points tenaciously to the pavement, and accumulating at compound interest.

Raven read on to the end of the chapter before directing his students to leave their chairs and find spaces on the floor. They were to close their eyes and, once they had done so, he redirected them to the opening paragraph.

'You are now going to leave Switzerland and this century, and, having done so, you must find yourself in Dickensian London. What do you see? You see – you must see – the fog and, despite the fog, also the mud, the horses and the umbrellas. And there is the megalosaurus, a fierce, two-legged dinosaur, with tiny arms, but a large head and a terrifying range of teeth. Its head sways from side to side as it races down Holborn. What do you hear? The barking of dogs, the neighing of horses, the squelching of mud and, perhaps some screams at the sight of the megalosaurus. What do you feel, taste and smell? Your legs stick in the mud, the moist air is on your lips, and you can smell the horse shit in the streets. What do you feel? Perhaps your umbrella clutched in your hand and the itching of your scarf on your neck. Now you are, or should be, in the London of Charles Dickens.'

'So what? If we stopped there, this exercise in visualising a scene which does not exist and never did exist would have no point. It would be a mere television version of a literary masterpiece. Keep your eyes closed! Eyes closed! There is no book in front of you. It is you who are inside the book. Now, remaining where you should be, on a muddy street in nineteenth-century London, and this is the point, you must interrogate yourself about your response to the situation. Are you really worthy to be there? Are you sure you fully understand the implications of the scene that Dickens has set out before you? Finding yourself in this situation, should you weep, laugh or yawn? It is not Dickens who is being subjected to your examination, but rather you who are being tried by Dickens. Good spirits may guide you to know your judge better, but bad spirits will surely seek to blunt your sensibilities and foster misunderstandings so that you fail the test of *Bleak House*.'

There followed an awkward quarter-hour's silence before Raven told them that they might open their eyes and resume their seats.

'Now you know what understanding literature through total immersion is like.'

Actually, this was not quite true. Lancelyn had had quite

a lot of difficulty in visualising fog and then a little later the megalosaurus. And, more important, his mind kept drifting. Was this visualisation exercise a kind of joke? Did Ignatius of Loyola read novels in this way? Was everybody else keeping their eyes shut? What was for lunch? And of course, if he thought about how hard he was concentrating, then he was not concentrating on what he should have been concentrating. So his visualisation of the Victorian scene was a thing of wraiths and tatters, all dimly glimpsed in a great darkness. But Raven then repeated the reading of the first chapter and forced them again and again to sit on the floor with their eyes closed as they worked through this scene and later scenes in *Bleak House*. Only on the fourth day did they switch to performing the same sort of exercises on selected sections of *Northanger Abbey*. By then Lancelyn had already had a dream in which he found himself to be a character in *Bleak House*, but one who had forgotten all his lines, so that the other characters looked at him impatiently before turning their backs on him and managing as best they could without whatever it was that he was supposed to say. Meanwhile he was looking for somewhere to piss.

At the end of it all Lancelyn and Bernard had been brought to repent their careless readings, their anachronistic assumptions and their complacently egoistic value judgements. They had been shriven by literature. A whole week on just two novels! But it changed the way they read forever. For example, when Lancelyn in Cannes had got around to reading Ian Fleming's *Casino Royale*, he as a matter of habit entered the novel he was reading, and he found himself with a glass of martini in his hand in the casino in Royale-les-Eaux, standing behind James Bond and staring down on the cards Bond had in his hand

71

during the opening round of a high-stakes game of baccarat. Lancelyn had looked round the casino and at first admired the novel that he found himself in. What is more, he had come to know the look, the smell and the feel of that casino more thoroughly than Fleming ever did. Only in retrospect did he realise that there had been another figure also standing behind Bond and that was Saint Ignatius, who was contemplating the hellish nature of what was going on in the casino. There was no need for Ignatius to say anything. They were both standing behind a gambler, a fornicator and a murderer.

How would it be now for Bernard at All Souls? In the evening everyone would be formally dressed and in their academic robes. Sherry or gin and tonic would be offered first. Then proceeding to the dining hall, there would be an array of glasses glittering in the candlelight, ready for a succession of carefully chosen wines. The servants would bring mock turtle soup, then lobster thermidor, then raspberry syllabub. The servants would also present silver finger bowls between courses. Of course at table one must not mention work or women. But perhaps the talk might be of university politics, the need to visit Wurzburg in order to see the Tiepolo frescoes, the latest novels by Robbe-Grillet and Mario Tobino, the merits or not of Harold Macmillan's Chancellorship of the University, Sir Maurice Bowra's latest witticism, Fellini's *La Dolce Vita* and where did the best cherries and cheeses come from. And there would be Bernard, quite in his element, holding forth about the importance of spats, as well as the names of the best librettists of New York musicals and how to judge a good Bordeaux. The diners would eventually decamp to an adjoining room for a second round of dessert. There would be cheese, biscuits, fruit and chocolate truffles. The flasks of port, sauterne and claret, would circulate whichever way they were supposed to circulate, and so would a silver snuff box. Finally coffee would be served together perhaps with a whisky, or a Cointreau. Naturally, the whole thing was steeped in tradition.

This was all in Lancelyn's mind as he picked at his salad in the St Andrews staff common room, which at lunchtime doubled as the staff canteen. Here the conversation, which he avoided as much as possible, was only about work. If only Iron Foot Jack had been able to turn up at one of the All Souls special guest nights. 'Posh nosh! This is a reel relish!' A servant would have to remind him to remove his hat. 'Nah,' to the proffered Bordeaux. 'I'll 'ave a pint 'o wallop.' Then Jack, unfazed by the distinguished company and indeed wearied of their tittle-tattle, would seek to lead their conversation on to 'igher fings and would keep his fellow diners on tenter 'ooks, as he described wot 'appened to folk once they were pushin' up the daises and approaching 'eaven or 'ell. Lots of people have kicked the bucket an' don' know it... this fantasy continued to sustain Lancelyn throughout the remainder of his meagre lunch in the common room. It was odd how often he thought of Jack. It was as if the man, discontented with his lot as one of the deceased, was trying to make contact through him with the world of the living.

Bernard was a poor correspondent and during that term Lancelyn received just one postcard from him. It listed various strange continental writers that he was now reading, promised to come up and visit St Andrews as soon as he could, and, before signing off with a 'toodle-pip!', concluded with the self-congratulatory reflection that, in a way, being a Fellow at All Souls was almost as good as being a member of the Bullingdon Club.

Three years earlier Bernard and Lancelyn's first meeting had been at the Freshers' Fair in the week before the term properly began and Bernard had been looking for the stand of the Bullingdon Club, so that he could put his name down on their waiting list, but there was no such stand and no such waiting list. Lancelyn was able to put him right about that.

'I think that you are looked over and then, if you look like the right sort of person, you will be approached. I think they are pretty cagey and, when they do make an approach, you won't have a clue what it's all about at first. They will ask you all sorts of apparently pointless questions.'

'Do you think that they might be looking over people at this Fair?'

'Er… I doubt it very much. I don't think they send scouts out to places like this. From what I have heard, they like to take their time over these things.'

As they talked, Lancelyn could see that Bernard was listening to him with eerie intentness.

'That is a public school accent, isn't it?' he said. 'I would like to talk like you.'

It had never occurred to Lancelyn that he possessed an accent. He had always presumed that he spoke Received Standard English, or some such thing. He admitted that he was fresh out of Eton and Bernard wanted to know all about that and he offered to buy Lancelyn a drink. So they went off to the Lamb and Child and somehow Lancelyn ended up paying for the drinks. After he had rambled on about sports, food, dress and slang at his old school, Bernard interrupted, 'I want to be like you.'

This was a bit embarrassing, indeed downright weird.

Bernard looked entirely ordinary, except, that is, for his face which was screwed up with determination. He had got to Oxford and he definitely was not going back to wherever it was that he had come from.

The next time they met, Bernard was wearing the first of his coloured waistcoats. For some weeks that followed it was a bit like that film which came out a few years later, *My Fair Lady*, but with Lancelyn playing the role of Henry Higgins while Bernard was a sort of stubbly Eliza Doolittle. Not that Lancelyn ever went to the cinema. He relied on people to tell him what happened in films, and from what he heard, he gathered that he was not missing very much. Anyway, without it turning into formal lessons, Lancelyn, through superficially casual conversation, drilled Bernard in the ways posh people spoke, thought and did things. As for the accent, it was chiefly a matter of keeping the mouth round as one spoke and of clearly stressing the consonants. But there was a limit to what Lancelyn, fresh out of school, could impart on the other matters and soon Bernard was learning more from reading novels, particularly nineteenth-century novels of what was known as the 'silver fork' school. For a while Disraeli's *Vivian Grey*, a novel about the education of an ambitious and fashionable young man, became his bible. Many other bibles were to follow, for Bernard did not regard reading novels as recreation. Rather they were supposed to give instructions on how to live. What otherwise could be the point of them? He came to place a particular value on *War and Peace* and *Anna Karenina* because those novels showed how aristocrats played cards, danced, ate, slept and had sex. When later Lancelyn tried to probe Bernard about his background, Bernard suddenly became suspicious and accused Lancelyn of being on a mission to assess his suitability for membership of the Bullingdon. At times it seemed as if Bernard was actually under the delusion that the Club was, like the Freemasons or the Illuminati, ever secretly present, observing, testing and working on a great plot which would take its members to their unknown goal.

Marcus was a better correspondent than Bernard. He wrote that he was desperate to get his degree over and escape from Oxford, since 'history is a nightmare from which I am trying to awake'. It was from Marcus that he first learnt that Bernard and Molly were going to get married. Though their formal invitation to the wedding, gold lettering on a stiff card, did come a couple of weeks later, the date of the wedding would be during St Andrews term time and Lancelyn would be lecturing and tutoring and consequently unable to get to Oxford for the event. It was all very well for Bernard who had no fixed teaching duties and consequently could get married when he liked. Lancelyn sent a congratulatory telegram.

Nevertheless they probably took offence and it was a long time before he heard from Bernard again. A letter from Marcus briefly described the wedding. As was compulsory on such occasions, Molly was 'radiant'. There were a surprising number of aunts at the funeral, maybe eight, though no sign of Bernard's parents. Lancelyn suspected that Bernard paid them to stay away and then perhaps he had hired actresses to impersonate the aunts. But Marcus had little more to say about that wedding, for he was more preoccupied with his own forthcoming marriage. As soon as he had got through finals, he was going to marry Janet, an older divorcée with two small children. Then he was going to find work – anywhere but in a university. After three years of living in the Middle Ages, he was fed up with it.

CHAPTER SIX

Four weeks after the first departmental meeting there was another. This time the problem of the cyclostyle machine was at the head of the agenda and this time Lancelyn paid no attention at all to the problems of its advanced technology and instead concentrated on his crossword. Then, looking up from the completed puzzle, he saw that someone else in the room had also been working on *The Times Cryptic Crossword*. It was a senior lecturer, the one who had been on the panel for his interview.

Once the problems of the cyclostyle machine had been thrashed out, there followed the question of on what terms aegrotats could be awarded and then the cost of binders for student dissertations. But the main item on the agenda turned out to be the literature of the United States. Wormsley wished to introduce teaching on American poetry and fiction in the hope that one-year courses on this would attract students from across the Atlantic. Since neither Leavis nor Lewis had had much time for American literature, this was briskly given the thumbs down by most of the department and Lancelyn took pleasure in observing Wormsley's irritation.

As they were coming out of the room, the senior lecturer took Lancelyn by the arm.

'I think I saw that you completed the crossword. Did you get (14) across, "Sprinter bearing singlet, one gathers"?'

'Yes, it's harvester.'

'Harvester? Oh… yes, of course. That is the way with crossword clues. They are always utterly impossible until they are solved, at which point they have flipped over and become blindingly obvious. There seems to be no intermediate state. Will you join me for a coffee?'

They had coffee in the little café in Market Street. Lancelyn's fellow cruciverbalist was called Henry Carleton. He was one of the leaders of the Leavisite faction and he detested Wormsley. Three years ago Henry had put in both for a chair and to take over as head of the department, but Wormsley had been brought in as professor from Glasgow and, furthermore, within weeks he had put paid to any hopes Henry had had of reaching professorial rank. Henry would grow old in this northern gulag and still be a senior lecturer when he died.

'When we knew that Wormsley did not want you to get the job, our minds were made up. That was enough for us and we all voted to appoint you. Mind you, I was uneasy about your specialisation in Browne and Burton, since I am a bit suspicious about non-fiction being treated as part of literature.'

Lancelyn was able to assure Henry that non-fiction was really a specialised form of fiction and that it borrowed strategies and techniques from novels and drama in order to achieve its realistic effects.

'You may be right. I never read non-fiction. I was young when I came here, young and ready for anything – except maybe lecturing on Spenser's *The Faerie Queene*. I was arrogant enough to think that this little town with its pretty beaches might be the theatre of my future triumphs. I thought… but what did I think? It is hard now even to remember. So little remains. Some library discoveries, some hopes of romance, then the increasing fear of the long winters, the snow, the darkness and the haar creeping in and, just once, something like an epiphany in the ruins of the Cathedral, a sort of vision of what I might become. But so little remains with me. Conrad had it right.'

And then, closing his eyes, Henry began to recite from memory, '"For me all the East is contained in that vision of my youth. It is all in that moment when I opened my young eyes on it. I came upon it from a tussle with the sea – and I was young – and I saw it looking at me. And this is all that is left of it! Only a moment of strength, of romance, of glamour, of youth… a flick of sunshine on a strange shore, the time to remember, the time for a sigh, and – goodbye… tell me, wasn't that the best time, that time when we were young… and sometimes a chance to feel your strength – that only – what you all regret!"' Then Henry continued more prosaically, 'Not that I have been to *the* East. The East Neuk of Fife is as far East as I have ever got. But I know Conrad and he talks to me. And you, you are still young and you must live and treasure your youth while you yet have it.' Then, looking at the undergraduates at the other tables, 'Now that I am at the age that I am, it just makes me sad to see so many young people coming up here year after year... so, anyway, if you can't bring Wormsley down, then leave this place. No. Even if you do bring Wormsley down, then, after that, leave this place. Look at me now. I am a scarecrow and a warning to you.'

Henry's warning made Lancelyn uncomfortable and he steered the conversation back to crosswords and soon they found themselves in agreement that the use of logic in solving the clues was overrated. It was even a kind of cheating and it was far more satisfying to use intuition in order to divine the setter's intention. But Henry was only diverted for a while, 'Somebody has to deal with Wormsley. I will support you. To those who barely know him he presents an outer façade of utter obnoxiousness and caprice, but that is merely a façade and the truth is that behind that unpleasant façade the head of our department is totally insane. Some years back he belatedly found religion through reading C.S. Lewis' *Narnia* cycle of children's novels and I really believe that Wormsley worships God in the form of a friendly, talking lion.'

They arranged to meet in the café at the same time next week to work on that day's crossword, but Lancelyn left the café a worried man. 'Bring Wormsley down.' How on earth was he expected to manage that? It was as if Henry welcomed Lancelyn as some kind of Antichrist figure whose arrival in St Andrews, which had long been foretold, would inaugurate the war against Wormsley, his lion and those ghastly children who came with the lion, and thereby Lancelyn would bring about the End of All Things in the English Department, if nowhere else. But, no, Lancelyn was not feeling all that apocalyptic. He was, after all, just a junior lecturer on probation. It also struck him that old men did not have a monopoly on the memories which made them yearn for what they had lost. Already the words of the Eton Boating Song were fading from his memory and he could no longer close his eyes and visualise the College's playing fields.

What would a character in a de la Mare story do in this sort of situation? Quite possibly nothing. De la Mare's fictions tended not to come to a climax. This ought to be right. Most peoples' lives do not have climaxes, for their lives just terminate without any such thing. Moreover it was not necessary for everything to be spelt out. Unlike stories, people's lives do not all have morals. Also a situation, however awkward, could come to an end with most things left unsaid.

Lancelyn had been reluctant to set aside entirely the idea of writing something about de la Mare and he had started a slow reading of the author's bulky novel, *Memoirs of a Midget*. It was the second evening of his reading and he had just got to the bit where M, the otherwise anonymous midget, comes across 'the carcass of a young mole. Curiosity vanquished the first gulp of horror. Holding my breath, with a stick I slowly edged it up in the dust and surveyed the white heaving nest of maggots in its belly with a peculiar and absorbed recognition. "Ah ha!" a voice cried within me, "so this is what is in wait: this is how things are;" and I stooped with lips drawn back over my teeth to examine the stinking mystery more closely.' But that evening Lancelyn read no further, for at that moment there was a thunderous knocking at the door. He had been so deeply absorbed in the description of the mole's decomposition that, for a very brief instant, it flashed through his mind that it might be Death at his house, come for him early.

Although the wind shrieked at him as he opened the door and the rain came down in torrents, it was a bit less dramatic than that. It was the young lecturer in the English Department, the one who had been at the Wormsley dinner, and the force of the storm drove him in through the door. Inevitably Lancelyn could not remember his name. The unexpected visitor helped him out, 'Jaimie Hay.'

And Jaimie extended a wet hand. Lancelyn shook it hesitantly, before taking his coat which was soaked and then leading him to the living room, which doubled as the main part of the library. Jaimie gazed with wonder at the books. Lancelyn offered him a vodka.

'Whisky if you have it.'

Lancelyn poured him a whisky and gave himself a neat vodka. Jaimie looked as though he needed a drink and Lancelyn waited for him to say something. As he waited, he thought I must get a grip on who all these people are. I have it! I will start a file-card index of everybody I meet in St Andrews: the name, date of birth if ascertainable, physical description, links to the university if appropriate, educational background, interesting conversational remarks if I am lucky enough to hear any, address and costume. I will start this tomorrow. It will be good for me. I never pay enough attention to people – except for those in books, of course.

Jaimie looked at most a year or two older than Lancelyn. He was slim, fresh-faced and had curly brown hair. That was not very much. How did one set about describing people? Perhaps one needed to look at a Dickens novel or two to see how one should do it? Still the silence. Was Jaimie in some kind of trouble?

At last he spoke, 'I have come on behalf of Professor Wormsley.'

'Ah.'

There was another long silence. Then, 'He wants allies. He needs your support.'

'Yes? He has a strange way of going about it. Why does he not come himself, instead of sending you?'

'He did not send me. He knows nothing about this. I only said that I had come on his behalf.'

'You will have to give* more help here. On his behalf for what?'

Jaimie did not reply to this. Lancelyn poured him another whisky and, though he did not reply to the question, that got him speaking again, 'I spotted you having coffee with Carleton a few days ago. I don't know how well you know him… it can be easy to ignore the fact that we are still living in the shadow of the War. The schools and universities are full of people who came through it, even though many of them did so horribly damaged. They may not have visible scars, yet still today they move among us as the walking wounded. He started teaching here before the War. Then, when it came, he volunteered and ended up in the Commandos. He was unlucky enough to be part of the detachment that accompanied the Canadians in the attempted landing at Dieppe in 1942. As I guess you know, that was a bloody disaster. The Germans were well prepared and there was a horrible massacre of both the British and the Canadians. Henry was wounded and captured and he only came back here after the end of the War. Physically he had recovered, but in no other way. He is really a ghost. There are lots of people like that and I think that, like him, they may not be quite sure whether they are alive and, if they are alive, why is it that they have been allowed to survive. Henry's book on Conrad, published before the war, is quite good, but he has published nothing since and his teaching is poor. The students can never find him in his office. Don't take my word for it. Ask the students. I also think he blames St Andrews for what he has become, but really it was the War. What did he say about Wormsley?'

'I can't answer that. It was a private conversation.'

'I bet it was. Slander is almost always a private thing.'

'Perhaps, but now Mr Hay I think that you had better leave.'

'Please, no. You should hear me out. My apologies for what I just said. I take it back and I really am sorry. I suppose that Carleton is an honourable man and you could say that I have just been slandering him myself. What I really wanted to talk to you about is Wormsley. He ambushed you during that dinner, didn't he? But you should not take it personally. That is his manner. The only way he knows how to make conversation is to attack and that attack is almost always unpredictable. He is like a Mexican jumping bean. He has so much energy that it can only come out as aggression. Whenever I see him, and before I can get a word in, he criticises something I have said or done. Then maybe, just maybe, once he has established his ascendancy, he can relax. He treats everybody like that, but, and it is a very great but, he is a truly great man and he will do great things for the English department, the University and, who knows, the country as a whole. OK, you could call him a *monstre sacré*, but it is the *sacré* bit that is important. Three days ago during the departmental meeting I saw that you just kept looking down at your crossword puzzle when the American issue came up. Doesn't matter. He will get the American proposal through with the Principal, the Rector and the Secretary regardless. The history department will probably also join him in wanting American students. So will Spanish and Scottish History. Putting it on the agenda of the departmental meeting was just to let people sound off. Departmental meetings never decide anything. But he is going to turn this department around and getting the Americans over here will be just the start. He is going to set up a joint honours course in English literature and creative writing. That will encourage the Americans to apply.'

At last Lancelyn was able to interrupt, 'What on earth do you mean? All writing is creative. Uncreative writing would be a bit strange, though I suppose the University could offer that as well. For God's sake, everybody who is not illiterate creates writing.'

'No, you don't know about this. This is outwith British academia. Creative writing is new. It is an American thing. University students are taught how to write novels, plays and poetry. Everybody has a novel or something else that is personal and valuable within them. They just have to be taught how to get in touch with what's inside them and put it into writing. It will be a great thing. We will be the first university in this country to offer courses in creative writing.'

'From the student essays I have seen so far, it would be a good thing if they were taught how to spell. But, beyond that, to teach a person how to be creative, that would be like trying to teach a person how to be subtle, or lustful, or melancholy. Surely you cannot teach an uncreative person how to be creative and there is no point in teaching a person who is creative to be what he already is. And even if they did turn out to be creative, they would be churning out novels and plays and putting them out on a market that is already saturated with the stuff. It is mad. If I understand what you are saying, then I would guess that this university would do better service to this country by teaching people not to write poems, plays and novels. Let their tawdry dreams stay bottled up. But, putting all that aside, I take it that Wormsley wants to set up a creative writing syllabus in order to lure American students over here.'

'Well, no, or perhaps yes. But mostly it is actually the other way round. It is the creative writing that is important to Wormsley and which should lead us on to our real goal. But having Americans over here will increase the demand for the course and so help us on the way to the big prize.'

'And that is?'

At last Lancelyn's interest was aroused and, keen to know this and to that end he offered Jaimie another whisky, but he refused and said, 'I think I have already said enough – too much in fact. You are too cynical to be told the truth. All I would say is that currently Oxbridge keeps picking off the best of our department, leaving us only with deadbeats like Carleton, but, if everything goes as Wormsley has planned it, in a few years' time not only will our department be cherry-picking the best of Oxbridge graduates and staff, but top-flight professors from Princeton and Harvard will be competing to come over and join us.'

Lancelyn shrugged. He would find out what plans

Wormsley and his talking lion had for the department and for the universe at large some other time. Evidently Jaimie had been bursting to tell him, but had remembered just in time that he was not supposed to and so Jaimie now changed the subject, 'It must be weird living alone in a big old house like this. It's a wee bit eldritch. I would worry about something strange in the attic or the cellar. To be honest I even feel uneasy now sitting with you in this room.'

Lancelyn shrugged, 'I have my books. I find that they are good company.'

'You should get them catalogued. It's quite a collection. I should say that you need a librarian.'

And with that, conversation became more relaxed and as it did so Lancelyn managed to elicit a little of the information that he would need for Jaimie's forthcoming file card. Unlike the rest of the department, he was born and bred in Scotland.

'They all want to go back to Cambridge. I don't. I live for the poetry of Scotland and the first place to find it is not in books, but in the mountains, the moors, the lochs and the sea. The books come after and literature should always be read out of doors.'

As for his literary tastes, he cared little for authors who were not Scottish.

He and Wormsley shared a taste for the stories for children of George MacDonald, *At the Back of the North Wind* and *The Princess and Curdie*. But his adult novels *Phantastes* and *Lillith* were MacDonald's chief claim to greatness, for they took the reader across 'a great frontier' into a world which, though very rarely glimpsed, was nevertheless closer to us than our jugular veins. And Jaimie enthused about other Scottish fantasists, notably James Hogg, Robert Louis Stevenson, Andrew Lang and David Lindsay. Lancelyn talked about his motorbike and his early difficulties in mastering it and then about his manic book collecting. Jaimie asked him about his researches into Thomas Browne's taxonomy, which was a bit awkward, but Lancelyn managed to talk airily about setting the learned doctor in the context of the seventeenth-century Scientific Revolution, before getting on to the more comfortable topic of the ghost stories of Walter de la Mare.

Then this all came to a rather abrupt end, as Lancelyn thought back to the dinner at the Wormsleys and asked, 'Who was that attractive young woman at the dinner a couple of weeks ago?'

'That was Sylvie... er, Mrs Wallace.'

'Was her husband at the dinner?'

Jaimie looked startled, 'God, no. He is dead. Somebody should have told you.' A pause, 'He was the lecturer you have replaced.'

'Who was he? How did he die?'

Jaimie rose from his chair, 'I really am not the person to ask about this. I should be going. I apologise for having dropped by without warning. You have got me talking and I think that I have said plenty already.'

Lancelyn did not think so.

On the doorstep, Jaimie turned to say one final thing, 'Wormsley does not like you, but what does that matter? Liking or not liking people doesn't matter at all. I have often wondered if, of all the disciples of Jesus, Judas was the only disciple to dislike him. Also, as it happens, I don't like Wormsley either. In fact I hate him.'

As he watched him go, Lancelyn wondered if he was liked by Jaimie. Probably not.

The following morning, before going off to teach he produced his first file card.

Jamie Hay

Age: 24? Education: Fettes and St Andrews: Status: junior lecturer in the English Department. Obsessed with Scottish literature. Appearance: handsome, curly brown hair, clear complexion, an elfin look, an outdoors look. More to follow. Costume: thick roll-neck pullover, scarf, raincoat. I can't really remember. What does he think of me? I am not sure. Somehow he seems to have a strangely innocent take on the world. Also, his obsession with Scottish literature is a bit much.

Well, it was a start. When he knew a bit more about Henry Carleton he would begin a card on him.

CHAPTER SEVEN

The following evening Lancelyn decided to make a proper start on the Browne thesis. It was one thing to immerse oneself in a five-hundred-page novel by Dickens. But the scale and eccentricity of the *Pseudodoxia Epidemica*, supplemented by Browne's other rather strange writings, threatened madness to their investigator. Nevertheless it was surely time to fathom Browne's taxonomy of error, since the sooner he could produce a passable doctorate on the subject, the sooner Wormsley would be off his back. So he should start by subjecting himself to the Ignatian method of immersion. He lay down on his library floor and closed his eyes. Having moved off from The Sign of the Gun in Ivy Lane, Browne's starting point, Lancelyn soon found himself at the beginning of a broad flagged highway whose stones were strewn with roses and myrtles and which ran between Amazonian tombs and temples, vainglorious pyramids, towers of silence, obelisks engraved with hieroglyphs, naphtha-lit altars, hanging gardens and funerary urns. He was in a city that was not built for the living but was for dying in. Beyond the light of the torches on the altars, the way was dark, for though the sun shone, its disc was no larger than it appeared to the eye.

He found himself walking beside the Archimime, the Chief Jester who of necessity walked at the head of all funeral processions, and the two them were followed by embalmers, their corpses in winding sheets, vespilloes, night-walkers, professional mourners, and finally, and keeping their distance, the resurrection men.

At length they came to a rotunda, which was the destination of the bodies, and on climbing its steps and pushing aside the entrance's heavy scarlet draperies, Lancelyn found himself in a tiered and marble-columned surgical theatre. Looking down, he saw the physicians at their demonstration benches which were cluttered with albarellos, apothecaries' flasks, philtres, alembics and bowls of fire. But the attention of Lancelyn and the students seated below him was focussed on a vast rotating table that had been placed in front of the benches. It was what Lancelyn would have called a Lazy Susan, though he had never before seen one a fraction of the size of this one. A corpse was carried in and carefully placed on the table. Now the demonstrator's aim was to show how the heads of dead men invariably became like loadstones and so magnetised. Sure enough the great Lazy Susan began to turn until the corpse's head was pointing to true north. This corpse was removed and another brought in and the experiment was repeated with the same result. Another corpse was carried in but Lancelyn needed to see no more.

Outside he found himself in the enchanted Garden of Remembrance, on the edges of which the burials of those corpses that had been experimented upon were taking place. But it was in this garden that nature sought to summon back its primordial past by seeking to replicate the original variety and luxuriance of the Garden of Eden. Yet, though what could be seen of the dense and teeming flora and fauna amazed the eye, time and again in this more modern age the generative principle behind this garden could be seen to have failed and, instead of producing living creatures, it had generated stillborn replicas in stone. So everywhere Lancelyn looked he saw fairy stones and disorderly mounds of seemingly petrified replicas or semblances of skulls, jaw bones, vertebrae, talons, wings, tree branches, bushes and small sea creatures. Moss was beginning to gather on the stony mounds of these freakishly figured sports of nature that sought to mimic living creatures but which were dead without ever having lived and so, among many such marvels, the resemblances of fish bones were found in profusion hundreds of miles from the sea. Nature was wearing out.

At the far end of the abortive Garden of Eden, he came to the Bibliotheca Abscondita, or the Concealed Library. The Library was there alright, easy to be seen. So why was it called 'Concealed'? As Lancelyn made his way towards it he wondered if its books would be organised according to the Dewey Decimal System. It was only when he entered, having passed through the catalogue room, that he saw that all the shelves were empty and that cables of cobwebs were draped over their emptiness. This library, if it deserved such a name, contained no books at all, because all the books listed in its catalogue no longer existed – if they ever did.

Now he was in Le Macabre and there was banshee music on its jukebox. He was confused and could not find the money to pay for his coffee. Had he left his money in the garden? But if so, how was he to get back to the garden? This was a cause of anxiety, but also very dull. And where was Browne or Ignatius? Suddenly things were so obviously dull that he realised that he was no longer in a true literary immersion and that he had instead drifted off to sleep and thence into dreaming, which was always a dull part of the night, and having realised this, he had no wish to linger in a phoney coffee house which was trying to charge him money he did not have for a coffee which did not exist and so he lost no time in waking.

He came to on the floor of the library. Even before the tedious dreaming had taken over, the message from the immersion was dismal, for in the world of Browne that had been conjured up, speculative philosophy had made its riot. Curse it, Wormsley was right. The phantasmagoria of rhetoric and metaphor that Lancelyn had just attempted to steep himself in could not conceal the fact that Browne had possessed nothing so rational as a taxonomy. The immersion had shown him a topography which was a kind of metaphor with long sentences heavy with similes and other vivid figurative imagery which, for all their pompous resonance, learned allusions to the mysteries and signatures of the sublunary world, and parenthetical doubts which were conjured up only to be dismissed, could have no other ending than a full stop. Lancelyn, who was not only not a Christian but also a hater of science, had been hoping to exploit Browne's simultaneous devotion to the Christian faith and his unsystematic pseudo-scientific enquiries for his own advancement. This could not work and the hypothetical doctorate was doomed. Foggy headed from all those baroque visions, he could not decide what to do.

Three days after Jaimie's visit, he met Henry in the café. They had both brought their copies of *The Times* with them and they settled to solving alternating clues. It was a companionable activity, but the puzzle was solved with irritating speed. Lancelyn pushed his paper away.

'It is interesting how often "imp" comes up, as in "impudent", "limp", "impertinent", "simpleton", "gimp", "impetuous", "pimple", "pimp", "skimpy", "improvident", "crimp", "imposition", "impostor". It is as if a perverse imp has found his home in the crossword.'

Then, though it was obvious that he should say nothing about Jaimie's visit, there was something he had to know.

'My predecessor in the department. Who was he? What was he like?'

'Michael Wallace? Has no one told you?'

Lancelyn shook his head.

'Well I did not know him terribly well. He was part of the Lewis faction. I guess that you know all about the Lewis versus Leavis feud in the department. A pity, but there it is and perhaps it keeps us on our toes. Anyway Wallace had a cult of C.S. Lewis – something that I can't understand. I don't care for Lewis' fetishising of Milton and his constant resort to historical contexts instead actually looking… but I better not get started on all that. I believe Michael was a specialist in the writings of Joseph Glanvill, a religious figure who lived in the seventeenth century. There was a big scandal about a lecture that he gave on Glanvill, but I don't know the details about that.'

'How did he die?'

'Nobody has told you! If I had been you and I had just arrived to replace the man, that is the first thing that I would have wanted to know… he committed suicide.'

It took Lancelyn a few minutes to digest this. Suicide was 362.28. It was in sinister proximity to sexual abuse, 362.76, drug addiction, 362.29, alcoholism, 362.292, and domestic violence, 362.82. There was a horrid logic to the numbers. Then he asked, 'How?'

'He went to the Cathedral and threw himself off St. Rule's Tower. I did hear that at the inquest doubts were raised about whether he had intended to commit suicide, but I can't imagine what those doubts can have been, since a lot of students, who for some reason happened to be gathered in the Cathedral ruins, saw him climb onto the parapet and throw himself off.'

'Is it known why he committed suicide?'

'Goodness. I wish that it was not me who was having to tell you everything. In a small town like this there is not much else to do, except have affairs. Sylvie, his wife, left him for someone else in the department, a younger man.'

'That would be Jaimie Hay.'

'There! There is something that you know! Yes, it was James Hay, a real charmer, but a bit odd, as if there were something missing in him. Let us talk about something else.'

And they did, though Lancelyn was so preoccupied with what he had just learned that he could not afterwards remember

96

what else they had talked about.

But now he produced his second card:

Henry Carleton
Education: Lancing and Pembroke, Cambridge. Employ-
ment: St Andrews English Department 1937? Enlisted 1939,
wounded and captured 1942, returned to St Andrews 1945.
Appearance: lantern-jawed, gaunt, worried, grey hair. Dress:
tweedy jacket with leather elbow patches. Publication: a book
on Conrad (maybe very good). Disposition: amiable, but
bitter about something. Not as good as I am at the crossword.
Dislikes Hay and Wormsley.

Whatever had been going on in St Andrews, it was surely not his problem. He had his researches to carry out and his library to care for and expand. Quaritch, Maggs and Fisher and Sperr sent their catalogues to him in St Andrews and during solitary evenings he mastered the vocabulary of the catalogues: *editio princeps*, foxing, Grolier list, dos-à-dos binding, primary binding and so forth. But this was a poor substitute for the hunt on foot and the hope of finding on a dimly lit shelf a book that had been catalogued and priced wrongly or not catalogued at all. So he waited for the hard winter to ease and counted the slowly lengthening days until he could get back to London.

CHAPTER EIGHT

Candlemas term ended on March 18 and that evening he took the overnight train to London and he was just in time to have lunch with his parents at the Café Royal in Piccadilly. He tried to persuade them to come up to St Andrews sometime in the summer, but they were off to South Africa and they had a taxi booked to collect them from the Cafe and take them to Southampton. Though they admired the fact that he was capable of getting and doing a job, they were puzzled that he had bothered to do so. Why could he not have been content to be a man-about-town? They thought that perhaps next year they might venture up to Scotland, even though it did seem a long way and presumably it was always very cold. He had also hoped to meet up with Bernard in Oxford or London, but he and Molly were going on a belated and lengthy honeymoon cruise down the Rhine.

After St Andrews the rush and turbulence of London came as a bit of a shock. As Lancelyn walked the city's crowded streets he recited to himself, 'I am the cat who walks by himself and all places are alike to me.' Since his supposed research on Thomas Browne seemed beyond rescue, he thought he might try and get some articles published on Walter de la Mare and to that end, having enrolled as a reader at the British Museum Library, he ordered some of his obscure early publications. Though he spent most of a day going through the early poems and short stories, he found it hard to concentrate, since he had the distinct feeling that something sinister had happened not far from where he sat in the Round Reading Room. It was only towards the end of his afternoon's research that it suddenly came to him that the vague thing that had until then been hovering beyond his recall was nothing real, but a fictional incident. A Mr Dunning had ordered some books to be brought to him in the Reading Room 'and he was settling the one he wanted first upon the desk, when he thought he heard his own name whispered behind him. He turned round hastily, and in doing so, brushed his little portfolio of loose papers on to the floor.' He bent to gather up the spilled papers and he was helped by a nearby stranger who handed him some more of those papers saying, 'May I give you this? I think it should be yours.' Seemingly a thoroughly trivial and harmless incident, but it was in this manner that the evil Mr Karswell was able to palm off the runes, which were ancient Germanic ideograms with mysterious powers, on the unsuspecting Dunning in M.R. James' ghost story 'Casting the Runes'. Dunning would die horribly unless he could find a way of returning the accursed runes, strangely inscribed pieces of paper, to Karswell in such a way that he would accept them – and with them the slaughterous rage of the Demon. Ridiculous. And it was a relief to have tracked the ominous subject matter down to a piece of fiction. But even so, Lancelyn took care not to drop any of his notes as he cleared his desk in preparation for leaving the Museum. Absolutely ridiculous.

Then, after the day in the British Museum and on his way to Soho to stock up with pornographic magazines and Black Russian cigarettes to take back to Scotland, he made an unexpected discovery. Near the top of Charing Cross Road, on the left-hand side, he came across Better Books, a small bookshop that he had never noticed before. He went inside. Though some of the books were familiar, the general feel of the stock had a strange and unsettling feel: the works of Aleister Crowley and other magical texts, guides to squatting and to mushroom picking, books on Red Indian rituals, manuals on drug taking, anarchist manifestoes, tattooing, Bohemian poetry, homeopathy, lots of Tolkien, books on Buddhism, yoga and tantric sex and Esalen (whatever that was). Taken individually the books were perhaps harmless, but cumulatively they were ominous and made him want to leave as quickly as possible, for he had a vague feeling that on those shelves the world that he lived in and was comfortable with was being placed under threat. His subsequent foraging in Soho's porn shops was more soothing, since the smiling, scantily dressed women in the pictures did not seem to pose any threat to his future.

The following day it was time once more for a descent upon London's second-hand bookshops. There was a horrible urgency in the mad hunt that took him from bookshop to bookshop. He experienced this hunt as a kind of rescue archaeology, for his sense was that he had been born just ten years too late. As a schoolboy coming up to London from Eton, he remembered seeing the most wonderful books on the shelves of the grand antiquarian book dealers. On one visit to Quaritch, he had found a copy of the Aldine Press edition of *Erotemeta cum interpretatione Latina* priced at ninety-nine guineas. Yet, though he had then been relatively flush with pocket money, he could not quite afford this treasure. If he had now found that same edition at five times that price, he would have wept with pleasure to have got it so cheap. And ten years ago or perhaps just a few years earlier, so soon after the end of the War, the former contents of many great country house libraries were flooding onto the market, but that sort of thing was all over now. And there was another aspect to the hurtling passage of time. Lancelyn's rule of thumb was that he might find one or two wonderful things on his first visit to a particular second-hand bookshop, but on his second visit the stock was never so good and on his third visit the shop was likely to have gone out of business. The smaller and seedier second-hand bookshops seemed to have the lifespan of butterflies and their proprietors were almost always miserable looking fellows, probably only too well aware that their enterprise was doomed. The shops, like mirages, just vanished. In the course of his mad hunts he liked to invent books that had never existed, in the hope that just thinking about a particular book might bring it into existence. Just once so far had this ploy succeeded and he had walked out of a scruffy bookshop just off Holborn clutching a copy of *Comment gagner aux jeux de cartes* by the Comte de St. Germain.

CHAPTER NINE

Back in St Andrews in early April, there was a postcard from Bernard waiting for him,

'I would wish you were here, except that I am a bit vague where we are. There is so much forest and so many castles and cathedrals. No wonder Germany lost the War. Most of them seem to be still living in the Middle Ages. We hope to get up to Scotland soon. Molly sends her love. Toodle-pip! Bernard.'

Two days later Lancelyn first met Quentin Mallow. Quentin was white-faced with long unkempt dark hair and wore his academic gown. (He always wore his gown.) From his appearance he might have been some kind of ancient Celtic monk and Lancelyn had appropriately encountered him writing in the ruins of the Cathedral, close by the Tower of St. Rule. Lancelyn had seen him around town and had wondered who he was. Now the monkish man looked up from his notes and, seeing Lancelyn, extended his hand, saying, '"Bare ruin'd choirs, where late the sweet birds sang." Hello. I am Quentin Mallow. You are newish in the English Department aren't you? And you are a Merton man. I was at Merton too, though a bit before your time and I read history. Did you ever happen to get to know either of my teachers, Ralph Davis or Roger Highfield?'

Lancelyn shook his head.

'No, but I suppose you must have encountered that strange Raven.'

'He was one of my tutors.'

'I don't envy you. He used to give me the creeps.'

'He was fine.'

'Really? Whenever I saw him I used to think of those lines of Edgar Allen Poe:

> 'Ghastly grim and ancient Raven
> Wandering from the Nightly shore –
> Tell me what thy lordly name is
> On the Night's Plutonian shore!
> Quoth the Raven "Nevermore"!'

'He was fine. He was a good teacher, but otherwise just ordinary.'

'Oh well... but someone told me, maybe one of my tutors, maybe someone else, that there was a mystery about his background and how he had ever been appointed. There is no record of him ever having been at any university, or for that matter, school. He seems to have materialised out of nowhere.'

Lancelyn shrugged, 'I never knew that.'

'Well, it does not matter.'

And Quentin went on to talk about his own work. His specialist subject was late medieval and Tudor chantry chapels. But he was here taking notes in the Cathedral, because the Scottish Tourist Board had asked him to produce a small guide to what was left of it. It was easy enough to see where the nave and transepts were and the same was true for the monastic buildings to the south of the Cathedral proper, but Quentin wanted to produce more than a dry description of the outline of the remaining stones. He wanted people who read his booklet to see how the place must have been in its heyday. In a sense, his mission was to wake the past and make the dead live again. But for today his communing with the ruins was finished and he proposed that they go for a drink together.

Having settled in the back bar of The Star, they talked about Merton matters, particularly the college's rowing achievements. But then Quentin was delighted to be able to get to know someone from the English Department, where of course most of the lecturers were ex-Cambridge. The History Department, on the other hand, was Oxford in exile and it was practically the rule among them that every evening one or other of their number should ring someone in Oxford to get the latest gossip from the fount of all wisdom.

'Of course, someone who has ended up in Cambridge will always have a bit of a chip on his shoulder,' said Quentin. 'So I just don't know the people in your Department. I have met Wormsley a couple of times, but on both occasions he was rude to me. I don't know why.'

'Did you know Michael Wallace?'

'No, not to talk to, though I did attend his last lecture.'

'There was a scandal about his death, wasn't there? Tell me.'

'You are asking a lot of me... that was quite a strange business,' and Quentin hesitated again before continuing, 'I don't usually go to lectures of other members of staff, but I thought I might learn something from Wallace's talk. It was on a seventeenth-century clergyman called Joseph Glanvill. My scholarly stamping ground is religious affairs in fifteenth-and-sixteenth-century England and I thought that it might be good for me to learn a little about what things were like after the sorts of things I specialise in were over. So I went to the big lecture theatre, crept in and took a seat at the back where I hoped that I would not be noticed. The audience consisted of second-year English students who were reading English with whatever was their other subject. So it was a big turnout of about one hundred and sixty, I would guess.

'At first it was dull and I was feeling rather sorry for the students, never mind for myself. I even thought that, if I could manage it without causing too much inconvenience to those sitting in the same row as me, I might slip away. We learned that Glanvill was a rector in Bath and he wrote *The Vanity of Dogmatizing*, which was an attack on scholastic philosophy, also *Lux Orientalis*, which argued for the pre-existence of souls, and finally *Saducismus Triumphatus*. The students, who were taking down what he was saying in the mindless way that students do, looked faintly bored. I don't think that there were many in his audience who even knew what scholastic philosophy was, never mind those Latin titles. He said a bit about *The Vanity of Dogmatizing* which had a much longer title, which I could not possibly remember, and then something about the theological implications of people having souls before they were born, but it was plain that he was hurrying on to the third book.

I remember the full title of this third book because I thought that in his craziness he might have been making the whole thing up, but no. I looked it up later and the full title was *Saducismus Triumphatus, or the Full and Plain Evidence Concerning Witches and Apparitions, The First Part treating of their Possibility and the Second of their Real Existence*. I believe that Saducees are mentioned in the New Testament, but never mind that. As far as Glanvill and the wretched Wallace were concerned, a Saducee was someone who denied the possibility of an afterlife. But witches and ghosts were real and their reality in turn testified to the reality of an afterlife. But then to deny the reality of witches and ghosts had to be a form of atheism and a damnable form at that. Then things got a bit strange – I mean stranger than they already were. If only I had had the gumption to stop the proceedings there and then – if only – but I had no idea how things would turn out.

Wallace told the students that he was quite sure that many of them were Saducees and, not only that, but in doubting the reality of the afterlife, they were in dire risk of eternal damnation, but by divine dispensation, he was here to save them. Then he threw out his scholar's gown behind him so that it seemed to be the bat-like wings of a demon. His voice deepened and it was as if someone else had possessed him and the lecture hall had been transformed into some kind of séance. He was no longer looking at the students in front of him. Instead he was gazing deep into the shadowy cave of Endor.

Michael told us that the prophet Samuel was dead and buried, but Saul, King of Israel, was still desperate to consult him and so he asked his servants to find him a woman who had a familiar spirit. The servants found such a woman in Endor, and, once Saul had donned a disguise, they led him to her by night and he asked the woman to raise his former counsellor, Samuel from the dead. And when the woman saw the spirit of Samuel and at the same time realised that the man in disguise who had asked her to raise this spirit was the ill-fated Saul, she screamed (and Wallace screamed). Though Saul demanded help from Samuel, the spirit could only tell him that God had rejected him and that he and his sons would die on the following day. Plainly, to deny the reality of the Witch of Endor was to deny the truth of the Bible and to deny the truth of the Bible was to cease to be a Christian and to cease to be a Christian meant eternal damnation.

Now Wallace was shouting at the top of his voice, 'I see many before me who are smiling, smirking, yawning to hear of the Witch of Endor. I see many before me who are irretrievably damned. I see seats in this lecture theatre that seem empty, yet they are occupied by invisible demons. I see that most of you are thinking that you are not so credulous as to believe in this witch in her cave, but I tell you that the only way you can attain salvation is to become credulous. I see that it is only with the credulous faith of a little child that you *may* be saved. Throughout life each man or woman is accompanied by two angels and they will control life's end. Though I have been abandoned by my most beloved angel, my other angel is still here close beside me and I am assured by him that I shall be saved. Blessedly credulous, I do believe and so I shall be saved. Now follow me! You shall behold a wonder! For as Glanvill tells us, "man doth not yield himself to the angels, nor unto death utterly, save only through the weakness of his feeble will". If only you will believe, you may live forever. You will see!'

In reproducing the manner of Michael's oration, Quentin's own voice had become loud and the barman was eyeing the pair of them curiously. Lancelyn put his hand on Quentin's sleeve and so then he continued more quietly, 'With that, he jumped down from the platform and, as he marched towards the door, he shouted again, 'Follow me!' and then at the doorway, Michael turned and repeated Glanvill's saying, 'man doth not yield himself to the angels, nor unto death utterly, save only through the weakness of his feeble will'. Though his voice was confident, even from where I sat, I could see that he was afraid of something. Then he was gone. There were, of course, a fair number of wee Marys in the audience and some of them were screaming. The girl next to me was sobbing, but I had to push past her regardless. At the end of the opposite aisle I noticed one young man on his knees praying. Of course I did not pause. I hurried out. Some students were following Michael, either to make sure that he came to no harm, or just curious to see what happened next. I had no idea at all what would happen next, but I thought I ought to get help. But from where? A couple of strong men to restrain him? Or a doctor? Or the police? I thought that perhaps the police would be best, but I just could not remember where the police station was. So I stood there at the top of Market Street and dithered. I am not proud of myself, but how could I have known? So anyway I did not actually see what happened next, for which I am now thankful. That tower... they really ought to close it off. Every few years or so a student chooses it as the prop for a spectacular suicide. But it is still left unlocked... you are silent.'

Lancelyn was thinking that, of course, the business about hellfire reminded him of that first Ignatian exercise which Raven had introduced him to a few years' back. But there was something else. The screaming students also reminded him of something. What was it? He thought it was an incident in one of the M.R. James stories.

Seeing that Lancelyn remained silent, Quentin continued, 'I can't think what possessed him – setting aside a dark angel, of course.'

'His wife had left him.'

'I didn't know that. Nobody tells me anything.'

When Lancelyn got home, he took *The Ghost Stories of M.R. James* down from its shelf and soon found the pages he had been thinking of. It was in 'Casting the Runes'. With apparent generosity Mr Karswell had offered to present a magic lantern show to some schoolchildren. It started off innocently enough with the story of Red Riding Hood, though the howling of the wolf that accompanied the slides was a little bit scary, but then the stories got scarier and scarier. The penultimate sequence featured images of a boy in a country lane and 'this poor boy was followed and at last pursued and overtaken, and either torn in pieces or somehow made away with, by a horrible hopping creature in white, which you saw first dodging about among the trees, and gradually it appeared more and more plainly.' At this point Karswell was ordered to bring the show to an end.

'All *he* said was: "Oh, you think it's time to bring our little

show to an end and send them home to their beds? *Very* well!"
And then, if you please he switched on another slide, which
showed a great mass of snakes, centipedes, and disgusting
creatures with wings, and somehow or other he made it seem
as if they were climbing out of the picture and getting in
among the audience; and this was accompanied by a sort of
dry rustling noise which sent the children nearly mad, and of
course they stampeded.'

Then Lancelyn sat down to compose a new card:

Quentin Mallow
Age: 28? Formation: Haileybury and Merton, Oxford.
*Status: lecturer in St Andrews History Department, specialist
in late medieval and Tudor stuff. Appearance: solemn, round-
faced, pale, almost Chinese looking. Prematurely balding.
Disposition: amiable.*

Then he took Burton's *Anatomy of Melancholy* down from its
shelf and found the appropriate passage:

'In such sort doth torture and the extent of his misery
torment him, that he can take no pleasure in his life, but
is in a manner enforced to offer violence unto himself,
to be freed from his insufferable present pains. So
some (saith Fracastorius) "in fury, but most in despair,
sorrow, fear, and out of the anguish and vexation of
their souls, offer violence to themselves: for their life
is unhappy and miserable. They can take no rest in the
night, nor sleep, or if they do slumber, fearful dreams
astonish them." In the daytime they are affrighted still

110

by some terrible object, and torn in pieces by suspicion, fear, sorrow, discontents, cares, shame, anguish, etc as so many wild horses...'

So much for Burton, but it was eerie to think of the voice of Joseph Glanvill calling out from across the centuries, calling on Henry Wallace to commit himself to the angel invisible beside him. Poor man! Lancelyn comforted himself with the thought that he had no fears of a similar fate, for he had his books to offer him company and comfort. Moreover he had no wife to shame and betray him and, above all, his dreams were not fearful. They were just bloody dull.

Before retiring, he looked once more at the compelling story of 'Casting the Runes'. After Karswell's manuscript on alchemy has been rejected for publication by an academic reader, the evil and vengeful Karswell manages to plant on that scholar a piece of paper with death-dealing runes inscribed upon it. But Karswell's plot is uncovered and, after the runes have been surreptitiously returned to him, it is he who falls victim to the demon summoned by the runes. It was a story that might give a normal person nightmares, but not Lancelyn who only dreamt of buses, lectures, shopping, pointless meetings and lavatories that were hard to access.

The next departmental meeting opened with good news. A new cyclostyle machine had been ordered and was on the way. Then there was pressure on the younger lecturers to offer new special subjects to the fourth-years. Lancelyn said he would be happy to offer one on Robert Burton's *The Anatomy of Melancholy* and its sources and influences. Wormsley scowled, but said nothing and it was not clear whether the offer had been accepted. Since the rest of the agenda was of no interest to Lancelyn, he turned his attention to the crossword, but today's was distressingly easy. So he opened the parcel which had dropped through the letterbox just before he had left the house. It was something he had ordered from one of the London dealers, a first edition of Walter de la Mare's children's book, *The Three Mulla-Mulgars* (published in 1910), but when he saw that Wormsley was staring hard at him, he reluctantly put it away, lit a cigarette and forced himself to listen to all the boring details of the new procedure for ordering books through the University Library, the provision of stationery for the end of the year exams, and finally a debate on whether students should be allowed to use the staff lavatories, which was as heated as it was tedious.

On the way out of the department Henry was waiting to check on the answers to the crossword with him, but Wormsley pushed Henry aside.

'On your way, Carleton, you and your crossword. I need to have words with this man.' Then, turning to Lancelyn, 'The crossword is part of the matter. It is an addiction and, like most addictions, it leads on to other addictions that waste a man. Look at Carleton for an example. If you want to fritter away your own time on that desperately trivial and addictive pursuit, that is your affair, but I will not have you ostentatiously not paying any attention to matters in hand during a departmental meeting. It is a discourtesy to me and to your colleagues. Is that understood?'

Was it indeed possible that addiction to crosswords led on to other damaging addictions like opium or masturbation? Too ridiculous! If anything, it would be the other way round, since

Lancelyn had masturbated years before he had started doing *The Times Crossword*. But never mind all that. He hesitated and thought back to what he had learnt about Wormsley from Jaimie, before replying, 'Of course it is understood, but it is not agreed. The solutions to today's crossword demanded very little of my attention and I was fully aware of what was going on in the meeting, which by the way, seemed to consist of a sequence of empty formalities. The Department's meetings never seem to decide anything important.'

And he turned away, hoping to catch up with Henry, but Wormsley grabbed him by the shoulder and said, 'Not so fast. You are easily bored, aren't you? There is one more thing. I recognised the book you were looking at. Unless I am much mistaken, it was *The Three Mulla-Mulgars* by Walter de la Mare. I think I recognised the cover.'

(The cover showed the three monkeys climbing up the tendrils of an unearthly fruit tree.) Wormsley continued, 'It is a wonderful book, isn't it?'

'I have not read it yet.'

'Oh, but then you have a treat in store! It is a parable of life's journey and how one needs courage, cunning and magic to complete that journey. The three mulla-mulgars are royal monkeys and they set out on a quest for Tishnar, which may be a land, or perhaps not even a land, for it is that which cannot be thought about in words, or told or expressed, and on the monkeys' quest, through forests, across rivers and up mountains, they encounter a giant fishcatcher, flesh eaters, and the deathly Nameless One who is named Immanala, and a capricious water maiden, and Nod ,the youngest of the monkeys has a magical moonstone which represents the power of the imagination, and the first thing… but I must not spoil it for you. Good reading! It is very exciting, though not as good as *The Lion, the Witch and the Wardrobe*, of course.'

So this was literary criticism and the sacred goal of Tishnar was effing ineffable. Lancelyn smiled politely.

Then a new thought struck Wormsley, 'You are not a Christian are you?'

Lancelyn shook his head.

'If you are not a Christian, then you will get less out of *The Three Mulla-Mulgars*, and for that matter, *Paradise Lost* and *The Pilgrim's Progress*. It must be disabling and sadly like looking at a painting in which you can see no colours, but only black and white outlines. I'm sorry for you.'

'I think that I see colour as well as anyone, and I have been trained to read and interpret literature and I have tried to read the Bible as if it was designed to be read as literature, but I do indeed find there is indeed very little colour in its narrative. It seems to me that the James Bond novels read much better. For how does the story of Jesus hold up as a story? The man's personality is only perfunctorily sketched and we get no sense of how he developed over the years. No scene-setting, no sex, hardly any violence. The secondary characters are scarcely sketched in at all. There should have been more tension in the build-up to the crucifixion and the enemy should have been made more sinister. And they arrest him too easily. And at the end of all this bad fiction I find that there is a feeling of… a feeling of… so what?'

'But have you thought that it might be a piece of bad fiction which happened to be true?' And Wormsley was smiling as he continued, 'You will make a very good enemy and that is something that I am going to enjoy.'

With that, Lancelyn was dismissed, but by the time he was out on the street, Henry had vanished. Sylvie had come to join Jaimie outside the department. She was very beautiful and they looked happy in the sunshine and Lancelyn once again committed her image to memory. It seemed that they were waiting for Wormsley, for once he had joined them and he had paused to point briefly at Lancelyn, they laughed and moved off.

Back home Lancelyn found a letter on the mat that he had missed. Marcus was by now approaching finals and desperate to be finished with the horrible business of history. 'The first time as tragedy, the second time as farce and then it's just more and more fucking farces and more fucking tragedies.' Of course, Molly would also be taking history finals and he had run into her in Carfax and they agreed that they were desperate to get out of Oxford as soon as the exams were over and so could the four of them, Marcus, Molly, Bernard and Janet, come up and visit in a few weeks' time and could Lancelyn recommend a good hotel for them to stay in?

Lancelyn replied that his house was easily big enough to accommodate the four of them and they must come and stay with him, and by the way, could he remind him, who was Janet? A second letter followed. Janet was an interior designer, older than Marcus, divorced and with two small children. They were planning to marry once Marcus had got his degree and found a job. And Marcus still thought that Janet and he should find a hotel, since he had discovered that St Andrews was on the sea. Though they had planned to leave the children with Janet's mother, a seaside holiday would be perfect for the children.

So again could Lancelyn recommend a hotel, but Lancelyn replied that there was space for the children too.

That night he conjured up Sylvie in his mind's eye. Mostly the female images that he masturbated to derived from photographs in *Spick and Span, Beautiful Britons* and similar magazines. Among the junior boys at school it had been rumoured that masturbation was the sin against the Holy Ghost. Nevertheless the pleasure was so intense that he had masturbated anyway and waited for the Holy Ghost to strike. But He did nothing and so Lancelyn ceased to believe in Him and, with that, his belief in the Trinity fell apart and it was then inevitable that he should cease to be a Christian. But, as he continued to masturbate, silent and attentive spirits waited on him. From reading the classic treatise against witchcraft, the *Malleus Maleficarum*, he learnt that these were the succubi, female demons created from the sperm of those who performed the sin of Onan. The succubi harvested the stuff, which was a little like ectoplasm, and slowly they gained shape and substance in the eye of the imagination. 'The power of the devil lies in the privy parts of men.' When de la Mare wrote of 'the impossible she' that 'She is memory and strangeness, earth's delight, death's promise. In a thousand shapes and disguises she visits us', was it possible that the 'impossible she' was a succubus? Although most of Lancelyn's nocturnal harem was derived from the magazines, from time to time he added women encountered in the streets and elsewhere. Molly was its queen and there was also Sylvie in attendance.

A few days before the beginning of final-year exams Lancelyn was sitting in the staff common room once again dispiritedly contemplating the ham salad he had purchased, when Quentin came and sat down opposite him. After some pointless preliminaries about the weather, he asked if Lancelyn could point out to him other members of the English Department who were in the room and tell him a bit about them. This was embarrassing. Lancelyn was even now so vague about the other lecturers, what they looked like, their names and what exactly they taught.

Quentin was sympathetic.

'It sounds as though you may be suffering from a mild case of prosopagnosia.'

'My God! Is this something serious? You say it is mild, but should I be seeing a doctor? Can you catch it from me?'

'Relax. It refers to the inability of the sufferer to recognise faces well-known to him.'

Still Lancelyn was a little shocked to discover that he had a medical condition. He had always thought of himself as perfectly fit. Then, though he had not got very far with it, he told Quentin about the card index.

'Why that's marvellous! That is prosopography and it is what a lot of our historians are involved with these days.'

'What the hell is prosopography? Is this some other clinical disability, like, perhaps the inability to read handwriting?'

'Nothing like that. It refers to the collective study of individual lives and careers, together with family relationships and patronage connections. Lewis Namier adopted it as the methodology for studying eighteenth-century MPs and Ronald Syme has used the same approach for the study of the politics of ancient Rome. In years to come your card index could be a great resource for historians studying the social and intellectual composition of British universities in the twentieth century.'

Then a thought struck Quentin, 'Am I in it? The card index, I mean.'

Lancelyn nodded and was about to say more about what he now thought of as his prosopagnographological file cards, when Jaimie came over and asked if he could join them. Lancelyn gestured welcome and then took pride in introducing Jaimie by his full name to Quentin. But Jaimie had come over to show Lancelyn something he had just noticed in *The Times Education Supplement* which he thought might be of interest to Lancelyn. It was the announcement of a conference to be held in October in Edinburgh and its subject was 'Our Spectral Ancestors: Victorian and Edwardian Ghost Narratives'. Bernard was listed as one of its convenors.

'This is your sort of thing, isn't it?'

Lancelyn was still pondering this news when Quentin pointed to a novel that was in Jaimie's other hand. It was called *Lucky Jim* and it was by a man called Kingsley Amis.

'What did you make of it?' asked Quentin. 'I read it a few weeks ago and I was quite shocked by it.'

'I am only halfway through it and so far I haven't been shocked by anything in it. What is so shocking?'

'No, I suppose not shocking, just terribly sad and the title so misleading. It is called *Lucky Jim*, but perhaps that is intended to be ironic, for the Jim character had started work on what might well have been a brilliant thesis. Let me see...' He started riffling the pages. 'Yes, here it is, *The Economic Influence of the Development of Shipbuilding Techniques, 1450 to 1485*. Most promising, and surely a brilliant academic career awaited this Jim, but then the young fool throws it all up. I can see that there are jokes in the book, but the underlying story is really quite tragic. A most promising future thrown over for a woman. It is, like so many novels, something written by a smart Alec who has no respect for academic goals or civilised values.'

Jaimie was looking at Quentin with incredulity. It was as if he had blundered into a conversation with a Martian. But Quentin did not notice and continued, 'The late fifteenth century was an exciting time for shipbuilders. More contacts were developing between mediterranean and northern designers and carpenters. Also open sea navigation was becoming more normal. Maritime trade had expanded considerably and with it the tonnage of the ships, but at the same time shortage of labour enforced certain constraints on the dockyards. By the end of the fifteenth century the rig of a ship proclaimed that its master craftsmen no longer owed anything to the Middle Ages. Jim's chosen period is the age of the gun-carrying ship, a presage of modernity. It is a thrilling subject and this Jim throws it all away for some pints of beer and a few fucks. By the end he is a ruined man – but, I'm sorry, I should not have given the ending away.'

'Not at all,' Jaimie was polite. 'You have put the novel in an interesting perspective.'

Lancelyn had been examining the paperback and the quote on the back cover: 'A brilliantly and preposterously funny book.' *The Manchester Guardian*.

'But what are you reading it for, Jaimie? This does not look like one of those soul-stirring books you want to take out and read on the wild moors and crags.'

Jaimie nodded.

'I am writing a novel.'

Lancelyn repressed the 'Neither am I' that automatically rose to his lips. But Jaimie saw the look on his face.

'Oh, I am not writing a novel in order to see it published, or even finished. I have no wish at all to become a novelist. What I really want to do is understand how novels get written and, to do that, I think that I have to get my hands dirty and write one myself. I think of myself as a kind of anthropologist who is going to live with savage tribesmen in order to learn and understand their ways. You see, I want to get to grips with the creative process. How does one make something out of nothing? How does one learn how to describe the world, not as it actually is, but as one might want it to be?'

'So what will your novel be about?'

'Well that's it. I thought I would set it in St Andrews University. That would save me the effort of having to invent the background. So it will be a campus novel.'

'A what?'

'A novel set in a university. Amis, having written the first British one, somebody called Bradbury has written another university novel, called *Eating People Is Wrong*. But I think that the Americans led the way with what they have called the 'campus novel' and Mary McCarthy's *Groves of Academe* and Randall Jarrell's *Pictures at an Institution* came earlier.'

Were academics now going to become fair game for novelists? Lancelyn could see that Quentin was looking as uneasy as he was feeling himself. But what Quentin said was, 'I think using St Andrews as your prefabricated setting rather runs against your creative purpose. I think you should set your novel in Shanghai.'

'But I don't know anything about Shanghai.'

'Exactly. So you make it up. I can see it now. The sampans coming down the canal bringing fruit. The mandarins being carried in their sedans or pulled in rickshaws through the crowded streets. The good-time girls in their cheongsams. And here is a tycoon wielding his swagger stick to beat his way through the crowd. And there is an aged Buddhist monk collecting scraps of food in a calabash. Everywhere the smell of opium, sin and death.

Jaimie was evidently reluctant to leave his beloved Scotland, even in imagination, 'That's not real.'

'No. It isn't, but it is a bloody sight more interesting than the place we find ourselves in today.'

Since Quentin and Jaimie had each evidently decided that the other was bonkers, conversation was at an end. Lancelyn decided that he would give *Lucky Jim* a miss. He left the common room thinking about the ghost story conference. Doubtless he would get an invitation soon.

CHAPTER TEN

So then it was June and time for the arrival of his visitors. He longed to be with Bernard again and there was a different kind of longing to see Molly once more. They had all travelled up by train in the daytime and arrived tired and travel-stained. The housekeeper had prepared a cold dinner for them, but Janet's children were starting to fall asleep even while they were eating and she had to put them to bed early. Everybody went to bed early. The following morning they all rose at different times and there was little overlap at breakfast. Janet had brought food for the infants with her and so they could breakfast on Coco Pops. Following Lancelyn's advice, Marcus and Janet decided to buy a bucket and spade and take the infants to the East Sands.

Lancelyn found Bernard in the library examining a book which he put back hastily on the shelf.

Molly had not yet surfaced when Lancelyn and Bernard left the house. They decided to walk the length of the much longer West Sands, two miles out to the River Eden and two miles back between the sea and the dunes. The golf course, the dog walkers and kite fliers were soon left behind. Clouds scudded ahead of them and as they walked under a grey blustery sky they could fancy themselves the last men left on earth. Bernard started by asking about Lancelyn's researches on Browne and Burton. He supposed that Lancelyn had given up the idea of working on Walter de la Mare. But then Lancelyn described his attempt use the Ignatian method in order to enter the intellectual world of Sir Thomas Browne. Bernard was the only person he could talk to about his immersion in a seventeenth-century author's phantasmagoria.

'The whole thing was a disaster,' Lancelyn concluded. 'There was not even a ghost of anything so logical as a taxonomy in the mind of Browne. So I have gone back to doing work on the ghost stories of Walter de la Mare – though I am keeping that secret from my dreadful professor.'

Now surely Bernard would come on to the subject of the Edinburgh conference, but he did not seem to have taken in Lancelyn's last sentence. Instead what he said was, 'It sounds as though you, like me, are having doubts about the Ignatian method. I think that it can be intellectually dangerous. That time we met in Le Macabre was the first time I had ever set foot in Soho and it made quite an impression on me. I was in a foreign land. I was in Bohemia. There was the sound of jazz coming from an upstairs window opposite Le Macabre and the surrounding streets were so busy with barrow boys pushing cans of film on handcarts to Wardour Street or fruit and vegetables to Berwick Street, and sailors looking to be picked up and women leaning at doorways and shouting to one another across the street. Everybody was talking to one another. I was fascinated and in the days that followed I returned to Soho a couple of times.

'Then I thought that I might try and get a sense of what it had been like a century or more earlier. So I walked up to Foyles and bought a copy of Thomas De Quincey's *Confessions of an Opium Eater*. I read it enough times to internalise its contents, until I believe that I could breathe and speak as De Quincey breathed and spoke. Then I commenced an Ignatian meditation on De Quincey's Soho.'

Now Bernard closed his eyes and placed his hand on Lancelyn's shoulder as he continued to walk and talk, 'I found myself in Soho Square where I lay on a pavement and horribly aware of my hunger which like a rat gnawed at my belly and, in truth, I thought that it might be no simile, but that a rat who was really feasting on me, for the Square and the streets around it were full of those noiselessly scampering rats and it would be with those rats that I would have to compete for the scraps of discarded food that I might smell and find in the gutters, and so there was no help for me in the moonlight but to be walking and searching, though this was very hard, for my eyes were smudged with tears and London is a mighty labyrinth, most of its slums still uncharted by the mapmakers, and which thereupon propounded to me many knotty problems of alleys, enigmatical entries, and sphinx's riddles of streets like so many involutes and parodies in stones, mortar and wood of my own mental convolutions and confusions, and so, utterly lost and in despair, and moreover with no expectation of a consequential *solvitur in ambulando*, I walked with the streetwalkers, their ashy white faces hung over with hair like rats' tails and indeed they were hungry as I was (as well as the rats underfoot) until at one point I came to Piccadilly, where the lights blazed from the great houses and the thoroughfare was like a raging sea in which I feared I might drown, and so I turned away and walked back on to Golden Square, at the upper end of which was a house, the White House, and I was suffered to enter (I do not know why) and I found it to be a purported house of horror within which ingenious contrivances made coffins rise from the floor and skeletons peek from behind curtains, though it was easy to discover that this was all a charade designed to conceal the place's true amenity which was as a bawdy house and I thought that I should shun this place and, footsore though I was, shuffle on until I reached the end of my predetermined sentence… but at this point the décor of the White House had so powerfully reminded me of Le Macabre that I felt able to extract myself from De Quincey's version of London and I was thankful to be out of it.'

Bernard took a breath before continuing, 'So there it is. The weepy and despairing De Quincey was dangerously close to becoming my second self, but I did not come to literature in order to find myself a vagrant. I happen to have grown up in poverty and so I am sure that there is no real romance in it, even though posh prose and poetry might strangely choose to present it as attractive. So from then on I was finished with De Quincey and, what is more, finished forever with the Ignatian method.'

'But it got you your starred first.'

'Yes, but the Ignatian method can only take you so far.

The trouble is that one ends up taking authors' works at their own valuation. I now find that there are more rational and dispassionate ways of deconstructing literature. The Ignatian method makes you wallow in the words and the visual effects they create in the mind, whereas I now realise that I need to analyse what is going on in the pages before me. Surely, if one wants colour and excitement, one can get that almost nightly from dreams. They are gloriously inventive. "Dreams out of the ivory gate and visions before midnight", as your friend Browne has it. But I don't want to be so entertained. I want to think.'

Lancelyn was about to say that his dreams were always dull and not worth talking about, and most often, when he did have a dream, he dreamt of having lost the notes that he wanted to use for a lecture, or being late for a train, or some other minor crisis that would make the night more tedious than it already was. But then, since he was determined to get the conversation back to ghost stories, he decided to invent an interesting dream in order to get Bernard's attention. So he said, 'I rarely remember my dreams. But now, come to think of it, I did have a dream in which, as it happens, I found myself on the West Sands. I was alone on the beach and as I was resting close to the water I found a penny whistle half buried in the sand, and after scraping it clear, I blew upon it. Then I stood up and started walking back to town and soon after I did so I became aware that I was being followed by a figure that hobbled and wavered in the wind. No, that could be more specific, for when I looked again, and though the light was obscure, I saw that it was a man and that he was limping. It was difficult to be sure, for though the man seemed to be hurrying after me, the distance between the two of us was very great and did not seem to lessen, but I still felt fear and it was a great relief to me to awaken at just that point. This is the first time I have dared set foot on the West Sands since I had this dream.'

And at this point Lancelyn was careful to look back over his shoulder with what he hoped was a nervous expression on his face.

But Bernard perversely did not pick up on the obvious plagiarism from M.R. James' 'Oh, Whistle, and I'll Come to You, My Lad'. Instead, what he said was, 'Interesting that the figure who was coming up behind you was limping. It seems that Iron Foot Jack, who obviously made quite an impression on you, has re-emerged from your subconscious.'

Now Lancelyn felt a chill which could not be accounted for by the cold wind which was sweeping along the beach, for the dead man's appearance in his imaginary dream was somehow more ominous than if he had turned up in any real dream. Of course there were fools around who would declare that obviously the appearance of Iron Foot Jack in one of his dreams, whether real or imaginary, was something that had emerged from his subconscious. But they were superstitious fools, for Lancelyn did not believe in the subconscious. It was a modern myth, a murky fantasy underworld and one of the many inventions of Dr Sigmund Freud.

They talked on of indifferent matters before subsiding into silence. Bernard's face was sombre. It was no longer the face of a man who used to rattle on about kissing barmaids and knocking off policemen's helmets. Perhaps he should challenge Bernard directly about that bloody conference. No, that could wait. It had to wait, for the next thing Bernard said was, 'Molly wants to sleep with you.'

'What?'

'As soon as possible. Why not tonight? It was she who insisted that we come up to Scotland.'

Now Lancelyn would have liked to smoke, but the wind was too strong for that.

Nothing more was said until they reached Hepburn Gardens. Molly looked at Bernard as he came through the door and he nodded. Lancelyn hurried into the library where at last he lit a cigarette. Just as the danger of a certain climb may be its chief appeal to a mountaineer, so the difficulty of a woman is part of her sexual appeal. Lancelyn found them very difficult indeed. Another cigarette. Then, when he emerged, Marcus, Janet and children were back and despite the unseasonably dreich weather, they had had a good time on the beach. Lancelyn took them all out to Forgan's Restaurant for lunch. Dreams came up again at lunch, for Bernard, having briefly described the walk along the West Sands, went on to tell them about Lancelyn's dream of summoning Iron Foot Jack by blowing on a discarded whistle. Everybody was agreed that this was really interesting and they pressed Lancelyn to tell them another of his fascinating dreams. Since he was damned if he was going to tell them about something as boring as his dream of dropping his lecture notes all over the place just before he was due to start speaking, he felt he ought to invent something more colourful. So he told them how he found himself in a churchyard by night where all was peaceful, but then suddenly a grave opened and a juddering skeleton rose from it, which was scary, but somehow not quite real. Then the skeleton sank back into the grave which closed over him and all was once more peaceful in the churchyard. This was repeated two or three times before he realised that he had been shrunk and that he was trapped in a seaside pier slot machine from which there could be no escape. Every time some little boy put a coin in the slot he (and the little boy) would be confronted once more with death. Lancelyn's bogus dream gave Janet the giggles. She was a very giggly person. Also very pretty, with short golden curls. Lancelyn considered adding her to his nocturnal harem.

But then Bernard gave them all a boring mini-lecture on how the interpretation of dreams was historically and socially determined. The same dream experienced by a twelfth-century serf and by a fashionable lady in Freud's Vienna had two very different meanings, since the content of the subconscious was socially determined. Lancelyn shocked them all by saying that he did not believe that he had a subconscious. There was, after all, more evidence for the existence of ghosts than there was for a subconscious. At least some people claimed to have seen a ghost.

After lunch Lancelyn took them for a walk around the town. They paused in the ruins of the Cathedral and Lancelyn was giving them a short account of the suicide of Michael Wallace when Wormsley came by and they were all introduced to him.

'So you are Oxford types like Lancelyn,' said Wormsley. 'I dare say that you have come up to see how we manage in the provinces. Well, we manage well enough. Good day to you.'

And with that he strode off.

CHAPTER ELEVEN

That evening the children fed early. Lancelyn had invited Quentin to join them for dinner. This was cooked by the housekeeper and her sister: chicken liver parfait and oat cakes, followed by pork and haggis sausages with mashed potato and broccoli and chocolate cake to finish with. Marcus and Quentin did most of the talking – about Oxford and history. Marcus was curious about academic life. Surely he was right to leave it and look for a job in the 'real world'. Lancelyn, Bernard and Molly kept exchanging glances with one another. Towards the end of dinner Quentin told again how he had attended the last lecture of Michael Wallace and what happened after it. Then Bernard took it into his head to recite some poetry:

'On the road to En-dor is the oldest road
And the craziest road of all

Straight it runs to the Witch's abode,
As it did in the days of Saul,
And nothing has changed of the sorrow in store
For such as go down on the road to En-dor.'

'It is one of Kipling's poems,' said Bernard. 'He was warning against commerce with spirits, but I think it would be fun to seek out a spirit, maybe the ghost of Wallace, for what harm can his ghost do to us? And I should add that I do not believe in ghosts. They are merely literary constructs.'

Well, it was a way of passing the rest of the evening, and certainly better than playing sardines which was what Janet had previously suggested, and so it was agreed that a séance would be held in the library. Janet found the library rather disturbing and she paced about examining the shelves, before declaring that she did not think that the books were tastefully arranged. They did not seem to be arranged at all. Now she was in her element, 'You should arrange your books according to the colour of their covers in order to create a harmonious effect. I would have suggested that you organise the covers according to the colour wheel with white at the top and black at the bottom. But the colour range of the books you actually have is a bit limited, with too many russet-brown leather-bound volumes and hardly anything bound in purple. The best you can do is create islands of strong colours, Prussian blue, yellow and scarlet, that sort of thing, among all the brown. Oh, and you should buy forty or fifty Penguin paperbacks. They are very cheap and they would provide more variety of scale as well as lightening the overall effect without being too garish.'

Lancelyn thanked her for the advice, but privately decided

that, when he could find the time, he would of course organise them according to the Dewey Decimal System. But then how could one use the Dewey Decimal System to classify such books as the *Hynerotomachia Poliphilii*, or a treatise on the *Voynich Manuscript*? The arrangement of books would be 020, library sciences. He doubted that colour coordination was part of library sciences.

Still the books certainly did need sorting out. Books which he knew he possessed would keep disappearing and, in looking for them, he found books that he did not know that he possessed, and then, when he had given up on the other books, they would reappear. His shelves were like the sea, constantly in motion. Bernard wanted to know if Marcus' books on coal and coal mining were shelved according to colour, but it turned out that Janet had made him get rid of them. Large format books on fashion, cookery and photography looked so much better.

So far north in July it never gets really dark. There is just a pearly grey light. Nevertheless Lancelyn brought candles into the library to create the right sort of atmosphere. It turned out that none of them had any previous experience of séances, but they agreed that, to start with, they would sit round the green leather-covered table in the centre of the library, hold hands and close their eyes, before asking the spirit of Michael Wallace to make himself known and then concentrate on making that happen. Quentin seated himself on Lancelyn's left and Marcus was about to take the chair on the right when Molly slid into it ahead of him.

'Michael Wallace, we conjure you to appear. We would have words with you.'

Five minutes passed with nothing happening. Finally, someone said, 'God this is boring isn't it?'

(But it was not so boring for Lancelyn, since he was conscious of Molly's leg rubbing up against his.)

'Can we open our eyes now? He may be standing silently in the corner.'

They opened their eyes. This was so silly. There was a general feeling of embarrassment. A couple of minutes ago Lancelyn had had a weird urge to burst out with 'I have a message for someone in this room', but really there was nothing else in his head except his intense awareness of Molly's close presence.

'What we need is a Ouija board,' said Bernard. 'You don't happen to have a Ouija board do you, Lancelyn?'

He did not.

'Anything with letters might do. Do you happen to have a scrabble set?' asked Marcus.

Lancelyn did not.

'If you want anything with letters, there is a tin of alphabet spaghetti,' said Janet. 'I brought it with us from London. The children love it.'

The tin was duly fetched from the kitchen together with some plates, forks and spoons. Now the idea was to take turns in dishing out a spoonful or two of the letters and asking Michael Wallace or any other spirits who might be lurking around if they had any messages for the assembled company. Quentin tried first, but nobody could make any sense of the mess of letters on his plate. Going round the table, it had to be Lancelyn's turn next.

UTAETLUEWHYLNADHOA

Experienced at anagrams as he was, he should have been able to unscramble those letters immediately, if only he had not been thoroughly distracted by the sensation of Molly's hand reaching for his crotch and fumbling for the zip. He might have thought that in these circumstances he would be incapable of physically responding, but this was not proving to be so. Meanwhile Bernard, who had been looking at him steadily, reluctantly lowered his gaze to the spaghetti and solved the anagram immediately.

'Shall I?' he said.

Lancelyn nodded and pushed the plate across to him. Bernard used a tine of his fork to rearrange the letters on the plate to make what could be their only message, which was 'WE ALL HATE YOU UNTO DEATH.' They all stared at the message saying nothing. Who was 'WE ALL' and who was 'YOU'?

'I don't hate you,' said Janet to Lancelyn and there was unanimous agreement about this. Then there was a prolonged silence. Looking round the circle, Lancelyn could see that they all looked embarrassed, but none of them actually looked guilty, and anyway, how could anyone be guilty of psychically manipulating pieces of spaghetti.

Finally Bernard came out with, 'Perhaps it is Iron Foot Jack. Remind me, what were his last words to you?'

'I've taken a fancy to you and, if you summon me, no matter when and no matter what the circumstances, put out the word for me and I will come to you.'

'Well that sounds a bit ominous,' said Marcus, 'but why "WE ALL?"'

'Perhaps Jack is using the royal "we",' Lancelyn

suggested. 'He was known as the King of Bohemia.'

No one was convinced by this, and as Bernard pointed out, Iron Foot Jack, far from hating Lancelyn, had obviously fancied him. Lots of people fancied him. Then Quentin came up with the suggestion that it was a general message from the dead to everybody in the room. The dead hate us because they are jealous that we are still alive. This was plausible, unlike the next suggestion which came from Marcus, 'Perhaps it is just the spaghetti letters that hate you, Lancelyn', and with that he collected up all the plates and the half-empty tin and solemnly said he was going to put the accursed spaghetti in the bin. When he came back from the kitchen there was another silence.

Finally Bernard said, 'Well Marcus, you certainly don't mince your words.'

At which point Janet was seized by a *fou rire*. The whole atmosphere of the séance, which had been at once childish and sinister, was blown away. Lancelyn used the moment to get his zip up again. They were all laughing and talking of other matters. He told himself that the way the letters fell out just happened to be a coincidence. But the night was young and there was still something for him to be even more afraid of. It was a couple of minutes before he felt able to rise from the table and offer drinks, though by God, he needed one himself.

An hour later he lay naked on his bed. He was trembling slightly. Perhaps this would be the night when he would lose his virginity. He had sometimes toyed with the idea that he might be saving his chastity for some sacred task, like Parsifal, Galahad or some other knight, but then thinking about it, they probably didn't masturbate. Less than half an hour had passed when Molly quietly entered his bedroom. She was wearing a black peignoir. She looked round at all the books that had overflowed from the library and said, 'It is weird with so many books. It is like getting laid in the Bodleian. I am going to get laid, aren't I?'

Since he could not bring himself to speak, he gestured that she should join him on the bed. She pulled the peignoir off over her head and did so. Sex scenes in serious novels were usually passed over rather quickly or else omitted altogether. He only wished that this was true in real life. She was so big, unlike the skimpy photographs of the women in *Spick n' Span*. Also she was naked, whereas the women in the magazines did not allow the male gaze to travel further up than their stocking tops. Molly's full body seemed to promise a plenitude of pleasure. She rolled on top of him so that her abundant hair hung around his face like a veil, and she pressed heavily upon him. Her eyes glowed in the dimness, and though she was smiling, it was perhaps a little like a raptor's smile.

'You are scared of me, aren't you? Don't be. I'm not going to hurt you.'

Then she pulled him over and guided him in. Just for an instant he had the mad fantasy that at last he had a real succubus on his bed and that the room was full of subordinate succubi who urged him on as he thrust away. Desire gave him the sense of conquest, which was at the same time the sense of surrender. Finally, there it was at last, that undistinguished thing. He had thrown away all hope of remaining a modern Parsifal in exchange for becoming a normal man. He found a cigarette and lit it.

'Why me? What's wrong with Bernard?'

What she said next almost made him swallow his cigarette.

'I don't like the way his prose style is developing.' Looking at Lancelyn's face, she saw that she would have to add some clarification. 'The way he writes is becoming too academic and that way of writing is eating into his character, so that what he writes, which is so abstract, so hedged with qualifications and so often couched in the passive, is beginning to mould who he is. The new Bernard is ever so careful to cover all his options and never to be caught out and, since he is also careful to be dull, he thinks that he will be OK in academia. Fuck that! It's not OK with me. But the hell with Bernard! I pray that you may never go the same way. What on God's earth are you doing up here? Do you intend to stay up in this Scottish hole forever? What is your goal? You are good at presenting the façade of a man of mystery, have you really anything to be mysterious about? It's hard to be sure. There *may* be more poetry, more soul in you. I sense a madness that I want to cherish. But then I could be completely wrong.'

Oh, it is the muse thing thought Lancelyn. Would she inspire him to write articles for magazines with titles like 'Does your man speak good prose in bed?'

But Molly, running her fingers down his chest, continued,

'Besides, you are much better looking. Bernard wishes he looked like you. This is a great body.'

'Oh, you know, I work out regularly in the University Library – stretching, bending, climbing, lifting heavy books, but they should have installed showers when they designed the building.'

She ignored this and returned to the post-coital viva, 'Who are you? Where are you going? What will you do?'

It was hard to think straight. He was revelling in the

smell of their mingled sweat and the dominant smell of woman. Besides it was his custom to give as little thought to the future as possible. He lived for the past and nostalgia was more powerful in him than ambition. Sometimes the wistful longing for how things were came so strongly upon him that he was hardly able to stand. Whereas the future promised the likelihood of old age and the certainty of death. 'The future is a foreign country. They will do things differently there.' But none of this was what Molly would want to hear, nor would she be interested in the fact that he was planning some carefully crafted essays on Walter de la Mare. He briefly toyed with saying that he was writing a novel. It was set in old Shanghai and had lots of tycoons and sampans in it. (A sampan was a kind of boat, wasn't it?) But no. Then he said, 'I have started work on my memoir.'

'Your memoir! For fuck's sake! You are what? Twenty-two?'

'Humph… why should old people have a monopoly on memoirs? By the time they get round to setting things down they are likely to be grouchy, pompous and forgetful, whereas I shall capture the freshness of youth in all its beautiful uncertainty, hope and sense of opportunity. The world is a mirror of my dreams.'

She looked doubtful, 'What are you going to call it?'

'The Prelude.'

'Oh, I like that. Will I be in it?'

'Of course.'

'Mmmm.'

And then it was time for more sex, followed by another cigarette.

'What happens now?'

'I will talk to Bernard tomorrow morning and, if possible, we will go back to Oxford tomorrow.'

'I thought that you might be leaving him and staying here with me.'

'They don't like me in Oxford, because I swear so much, but they all swear, so why shouldn't I? The hell with Oxford! I will leave it and him and come to join you here, but first you have to prove yourself to me. Write this *Prelude* and I promise you that I am yours. I believe you can do it. Raven told me that, despite your not getting a very good first, you actually are a genius and I hope that I may have now found out what I needed to know.'

So that was how muses operated! Molly probably wanted to give birth to a genius and he was going to be used – though in the nicest possible way. It was probably around five when she left his bed and presumably went back to Bernard. Now at last Lancelyn had really climaxed with a woman. As a lecturer in English literature, he was acutely aware that, after the climax, there could only be anti-climax and therefore most novelists placed the climax at or near the end of their books. Nevertheless, quite a few Victorian novelists preferred to place the climax in the middle of the book. But it was possible that he was getting his categories mixed up...

The following morning Bernard and Molly were gone before anyone else was up. Lancelyn told Marcus and Janet that Molly had had an urgent telephone call and that her mother was seriously ill. He did not think that they believed him, though they could not be bothered to challenge his lie, and Marcus hinted that he was glad they were gone, since they had seemed a bit on edge these last couple of days. Why did Molly swear so much? But Bernard especially looked tense and unhappy. Marcus hoped things were going well for him at All Souls, though perhaps they were not. And Lancelyn was wondering, why had Bernard agreed to come up to St Andrews in the first place? Something was going on that he did not understand.

Three days later Marcus, Janet and the children left for London and two days after that Lancelyn, thirsting for bookshops, was also able to set out from St Andrews. As the train pulled away from the station he felt a mysterious sense of relief to be away from the place, for he sensed that something in that quiet respectable town was making him uneasy. But the jitteriness came back when he turned to *The Times Crossword*, since he was now constantly searching for anagrams and fearful that, once decoded, their letters might carry some message of menace that was addressed to him personally.

CHAPTER TWELVE

Not only were second-hand bookshops the repositories of rejected knowledge, they were also refuges for rejected people – the lonely, the destitute, the dim-witted, and the outright mad, all non-buyers. Dangerous knowledge and mad texts also found their home in such repositories. In a shop in Marylebone High Street Lancelyn at last found his own copy of Kramer and Sprenger's *Malleus Maleficarum*, a treatise on the evils of witches and of women more generally. His library already included *The Protocols of the Elders of Zion*, Wierus' *Pseudomonarchia Daemonis*, De Sade's *A Hundred and Twenty Days of Sodom*, *A Treatise on Nabataean Agriculture*, *The King in Yellow*, Pisanus Fraxi's *De Liber Prohibitorum*, *Tractatus De Modo Cacandi*, *Mein Kampf*, Aleister Crowley's *The Book of Lies* and *Hermippus Redividus* (this last on the restorative powers of the breath of young girls). Such mad books were safe in his care. Also, on this visit to London, he succeeded yet again in purchasing an early printing of a book about which he had known hardly anything, except that it was blasphemous and that it had never existed. This was the *De Tribus impostoribus* by an unknown author. It was one of the rumoured dark books of the Middle Ages, for the imposters in question were Moses, Jesus and Mohammed.

His thirst for books somewhat slaked, he then decided to go up to Oxford to begin research on his recent past for *The Prelude*. Anyway, of course, there would be more bookshops to be searched in that city. He telephoned Raven and proposed to take him out to dinner, but Raven counter-proposed that Lancelyn should dine with him at Merton's high table and then stay the night in college.

In Oxford Lancelyn was fearful of encountering Bernard in the streets. On the other hand, he half hoped to run into Molly and then to persuade her to come away with him there and then. Raven had invited him to a quick sherry in his study before dinner. He wanted to say something that was not for the ears of those at high table. He was looking a little grey and his hand shook as he reached for the decanter. Once the glass had been poured and without any preamble he started speaking,

'I did not set out to become a literature don. When the war broke out I was in London and teaching mathematics at Imperial College. I was hoping eventually to switch to astrophysics. The war put paid to that. I took part in the Eighth Army landing in Italy, but some weeks' later got separated from my battalion. On the run from an elite division of the Panzer SS, I discovered the terror which is the beginning of wisdom. Fortunately I was picked up by partisans and they passed me from hiding place to hiding place until I ended up being concealed in a monastery high in the Apennines. Happily it was not Monte Cassino and I was able to spend peaceful months there. The clarity and silence of the place were extraordinary and I felt as though my body was being washed clean of all the scum of warfare. I used to sleep under the stars on the roof of dorter. But it soon became rather dull. Though the Cistercian monks were kind, they were not given to conversation, and since there was no secular literature to be found in the place, I turned with initial reluctance to the *Exercita spiritualia* of Ignatius of Loyola. Beyond the peace of the monastic cloisters, great things were happening in the wider world and the monks brought reports of massive destruction and deaths beyond number down there. So then it seemed to me intensely desirable to lose all care for the perishable things of that world. Ignatius' exercises helped me in this, as well as increasing the power of my memory, understanding and will – all in preparation for an ultimate encounter with God. Eventually and with regret I left the monastery and re-joined my battalion as it continued its accelerating advance up the boot of Italy. Explosions and screams replaced the sound of bells and the singing of the Hours.

'Back in England and demobilised, I could have resumed my teaching at Imperial, or I could have gone into politics. I had known Attlee, when he was just a major and there were others who would have been useful contacts. Instead I did three things. I arranged to be received into the Catholic Church, I changed my name by deed poll and I commenced the intensive study of Victorian literature with the aim of becoming an unrivalled expert on the subject. Mind you, in order to turn myself into that expert, I had to read some godawful novels – as you have done under my guidance. Books and bookish scholarship are so much vanity that pass before the face of the Lord. I could have taught anything, but I thought that literary studies would best serve my and His purpose. You see, I am the "Hound of Heaven". But now it is time for us to join my colleagues for pre-dinner drinks.'

If 'Hound of Heaven' had by any chance been Raven's original name, then no wonder he had changed it by deed poll. In the chamber next to the dining hall the fellows of Merton and assorted guests had assembled for drinks and the scrutiny of the seating arrangements. Raven introduced him to the Master before going off to talk to someone else. The Master and he had inconsequential conversation about recent changes in the college and about how four-year courses were managed in St Andrews. Then Lancelyn sought out Raven again in the cluster of dons. Raven had his back to him and to Lancelyn's surprise he saw that Raven was talking to Emeritus Professor Tolkien, who had presumably come up from Eastbourne to deal with something regarding Merton's archives, literary legacies, or bibliographic queries. He had not thought that Raven and Tolkien were on speaking terms. He did not break up their conversation but stood behind Raven and eavesdropped.

'Yes, it is in Tacitus' *Germania*. Signs inscribed on pieces of bark were used for the purpose of divination. Nevertheless, we cannot be quite sure that those signs were runes.'

That was Tolkien, who evidently was responding to a question that Raven had asked. Now Raven had a further question, 'But what about the use of runes for other magical purposes?'

'Difficult. My memory for these things is beginning to go. "If high on a tree I see a hanged man swing, so I do write and colour runes." That is from the *Poetic Edda*. There may be more that is relevant... if that is relevant. I just can't remember.'

Then Tolkien indicated to Raven that there was someone standing directly behind him and so Lancelyn had to be introduced to Tolkien and he insincerely told him how much he had enjoyed *The Lord of the Rings*. At that point the Master started to usher them into the hall. Lancelyn found himself seated between a young classics fellow and Tolkien. Raven was seated at the far end of the long table, which was intensely frustrating as Lancelyn had many things that he wanted to ask him, in particular there was something Molly had said. Nevertheless he and Tolkien did have an engrossing conversation about the editing of *Sir Gawain and the Green Knight*.

After dinner Raven wished Lancelyn a good night, but Lancelyn was not to be fobbed off, 'We need to talk some more. Some things puzzle me.'

Raven groaned. Then, 'Oh dear. Very well. But I am very tired and I hope that there are not too many things puzzling you.'

And so they walked past the staircase on which his rooms were located and continued to pace around Mob Quad. Then Raven, ghostly in the moonlight, coughed and gestured that Lancelyn should speak.

'Did you know that Bernard and Molly came to stay with me in St Andrews at the end of last term?'

Raven nodded.

'How did you know that and when did you tell Molly that I was more intelligent than Bernard?'

'Oh, I can't remember. We regularly have lunch together, a great pleasure and something I look forward to, for she is, as the common idiom has it, easy on the eye. If only I were not so old…' Then seeing that Lancelyn was obviously not going to be satisfied with this response, he continued, 'She values my advice and I wish to keep tabs on you and Bernard through her. I regret that these days Bernard seems to be avoiding me.'

'So how much do you know about what happened when Bernard and Molly were with me in St Andrews?'

'Everything I hope, but would it not be embarrassing for you and for me if I were to spell it out? I must say, I am most curious about your proposed *Prelude.*'

Lancelyn ignored these last words.

'I am sorry to say this, but this all sounds like some seedy godgame on your part. Did you know that Bernard has renounced the Ignatian method?'

'Oh, that does not matter. Have you read Chesterton's *The Innocence of Father Brown*? "I caught him with an unseen hook and an invisible line which is long enough to let him wander to the ends of the earth, and still to bring him back with a tug upon the thread." As for the godgame, that seems to me to be the only game in town. You know there are others I keep watch over, Sanderson in Freiburg, Bolton at the Pentagon and one or two others.'

'Why did Molly come to you in the first place?'

'She wanted to interview me about your prospects. As if I were your father! You must have gathered by now that she is very keen to attach herself to a man she can make something of. She puts it about that she has the strange ambition to achieve greatness vicariously. I am not sure that I believe this, but I believe that her ambition will destroy Bernard and that I regret. And then, if you let her, she will go on to break your heart before leaving you as well. But, but, and I say again *but*, that will be the best thing that will ever happen to you. It will be your broken heart which will make you fully a human being.'

Lancelyn did not know what to make of this. So he changed the subject.

'Have you ever met Professor Wormsley?'

'I did. Spikey fellow. He had a rather tedious hobby. Collecting postcards, or taking rubbings from manhole covers, or something like that. I can't remember.'

'His idea of using literature to bring his students to God seems a bit similar to yours.'

Raven shrugged and then had a fit of coughing before replying, 'We are toilers in the same vineyard. But I bet I bring in more souls than he does. Apart from anything else, his manner is so off-putting. Besides, his ultimate goal strikes me as outright blasphemous.'

Had Raven known Michael Wallace? What was Raven's name before he changed it? Why Raven? Was it a tribute to the raven which croaks 'Nevermore' in the Edgar Allen Poe poem? Or was it a reference to one of Odin's ravens that flew over the world as his spies? Had he views on supernatural spaghetti? What was Wormsley's blasphemous ultimate goal? Lancelyn was about to ask him that last question when Raven seeing that he was about to face yet a further interrogation, turned to him in fury.

'Must you have everything spelled out? It will all be fine. The pattern always comes right. It is just a matter of recognising it. Trust me. The year that starts in October will be my last year. I have done enough and besides I am sick – of literature that is. I hope that you will visit me in the future and we may have a longer conversation. But right now I am old, very tired and I need my bed. Good night Lancelyn.'

The following day Lancelyn wandered around the college gardens and into the library as he sought to commit to memory incidents from his recent past and the places where they had happened. Then the town's bookshops were also places of memory that had to be visited. Though it was certainly ridiculous, in between bookshops, he found himself checking shop fronts, road signs and menus for dangerous messages, though he found none. He needed to conquer his fear of anagrams.

A few days later he walked around Windsor and Eton where he struggled in vain to conjure up the full summery glory of his schooldays. Happy to be in England, he had been happier yet to be at Eton. Apart from anything else, his arrival there was just ahead of his discovery of sex, something that the curvy body of the Evil Queen had only hinted at. The junior boys shared master classes in how to masturbate under the showers beside the swimming pool. They also shared information about where to buy magazines like *Men Only* and *Windmill*. Before arriving at Eton he had had dim suspicions that there was something important that grown-ups were keeping secret from him. Now that mystery was over. OK. But suppose that, beyond this, there was another big secret that people were keeping from him. This could explain conversations that suddenly fell silent, newspapers with pages ripped out of them, offices whose purposes were inscrutable, all manner of things. There might yet be a *Mysterium Magnum* beside which sex might only be a *Mysterium Parvum*.

He liked being taught and the masters took more interest in him than his father ever had. He loved the hierarchies, rituals and special language of the place. In his first years he did not mind fagging and his prowess at rugby and rowing saved him from being called a swot and then being bullied. He gained an early reputation as a 'wet bob'. So things were fine and then at the beginning of his final year he ascended into heaven when he was elected to Pop, which is as much as to say that he became one of the lords of creation. He was one of only twenty of the College's prefects. Pop was the elite within an elite. Consequently he was entitled to wear any kind of waistcoat he chose, together with grey spotted trousers. He would carry a furled umbrella and sport a gardenia in his buttonhole. He was a swell. He was entitled to administer a Pop tan flogging and little boys were running scared of him. In the 1950s a vast part of the map of the globe was still coloured pink and as Cecil Rhodes had enjoined, Englishmen, by virtue of being English, they had won 'the first prize in the lottery of life'. But then: 'Farewell happy Fields Where Joy forever dwells.' If only his dreams would take him back to the College for a few minutes, but they never did. Eton had been a preparation for Oxford and Oxford had been a preparation for life. So now it was reasonable to ask for what was life a preparation.

Going yet further back, he remembered the ship docking at Aden on its way to Southampton. His father and mother had accompanied him on the long voyage to London to see him to his new school, but then his father had been urgently recalled to Teheran. It was something to do with a very bad man called Mossadeq, who was either about to make himself dictator of Persia or else he was going to be overthrown. It was not clear which, but whatever the outcome, its consequences would be momentous for the Anglo-Persian Oil Company (which only a year later would change its name to the British Petroleum Company). They had arrived in England the day Hillary and Tenzing had conquered Everest and just a few days before the Coronation. There was bunting everywhere and here and there he glimpsed street parties with flags and jellies (and he loved the Coronation mugs with their lions, unicorns and flags). Despite all the Union Jacks, London was drab and there were bomb sites almost everywhere. Lancelyn loved it. It was such a wonderful contrast to the virulent colours and sizzling heat of Teheran and the Caspian beaches. His mother had taken him to the school outfitters in Windsor and fully fitted out, he thought that he looked like the British Ambassador to the Shah of Persia.

Even now in 1962 there were still bombsites and colonies of prefabs in London. Not that much had changed since the 50s. Lancelyn was on his way to The Travellers, but for old time's sake, he stopped at Le Macabre. A year had passed and now a shadow line had been crossed and they were all grown-up. That last occasion the Dead March from Handel's *Saul* had been playing on the jukebox. He put it back on again to help summon up the image of Molly as she had sat opposite him on that day. He thought of it as their tune, the more so because it was a sad one, and as *The Anatomy of Melancholy* had it: 'Many men are melancholy by hearing music, but it is a pleasing melancholy that it causeth; and therefore to such as are discontent, in woe, fear and sorrow, or dejected, it is a most potent remedy: it expels cares, alters their grieved minds, and easeth in an instant'. Then there was the memory of the much earlier encounter with Iron Foot Jack. Or was it exactly that? Was it not the memory of how he had remembered Iron Foot Jack on previous occasions? The original direct memory of that encounter was receding further and further back and was forever beyond direct recall. The same would be true of his memory of how Molly was in the coffee house that afternoon a little over a year ago. He had the Dead March play once more. Then he had to hurry on to meet his father.

Since the flat in Albany was being redecorated, Lancelyn was staying with Marcus and Janet, while his father was staying at the Travellers Club and that was where they had lunch. His father had forgotten to bring along the photographs Lancelyn had asked for, which in retrospect was just as well. Photographs pin memories down and narrow their focus, so that only the precise images remain, while their context is lost. Memories adhered to photographs and became parasitic upon them in order to survive. But in the long run photographs replaced any genuine recall of past images or incidents and they removed them from the stock of memory, which in every human brain is constantly under reconstruction and development. Lancelyn wanted to talk about their memories of Iran in the 50s, but his father only wanted to talk politics. This was infuriating, for surely his father had more memories of him as he was in Teheran than he had himself. Mother was having a fitting. He never found out where she was staying. They would shortly be leaving for Valparaiso.

Going yet further back, Lancelyn had had a good war, at least as far as he could remember it. Life may be a journey, but it is a strange sort of journey in which it is quite impossible to remember where one started out from. Later he was told that he was born prematurely in Abadan in 1940. He thought that his earliest memory was probably of crawling over the large carpet in the reception room of the Anglo-Iranian Oil Company compound in Teheran. As he made his way over the carpet, he sought to follow the pattern in it, but he was always getting lost. If only his nursemaid would allow him enough time to reach the end, but she preferred him out in the garden where his pee could do no damage. She was Persian, dark-skinned, young and pretty. He learned Persian from her and he saw much more of her than he did of his mother.

He remembered collecting wisteria and cherry blossom petals and helping the tortoises navigate their way across the water channels that criss-crossed the garden. There was also a gazelle, though it died. He read *Winnie the Pooh* in the compound's lengthening evening shadows. Later he helped the servants in passing round the caviar sandwiches and kebabs at his parents' parties. Some months before the journey to England he had riding lessons. He also received lots of private tuition and he remembered taking the Eton entry exam alone in a locked room in the British Legation. Though he had still possessed a speaking knowledge of Persian when he arrived at Eton, it gradually fell away. These fragments could not constitute any kind of narrative. They merely provided reassurance that he had once been a child.

His last memory of Iran was a film he saw in an open-air cinema in northern Teheran. It was probably the first film he had ever seen and certainly the last. It was called *Snow White and the Seven Dwarfs*. Its story was fearful and rather strange and still, after so many years, he had not been able to quite make sense of it. It was the story of a proud and very beautiful Queen who is lied to by a magical smoky image in her mirror and thence led to her death. When she asked the mirror who was the most beautiful in the land, the demon behind the glass told her that it was someone called Snow White. But Snow White could be seen to be pale, slightly plump, insipid, and not fully a woman, whereas, when the boy that Lancelyn was contemplated the Queen in her tightly fitting purple robe and black cloak, he felt something new stir within him. But by magic (or could it have been just by the ravages of time?), she was turned into an aged crone with an attendant raven. So why did the image in the mirror lie to the queen? Was it in truth the reflection of her own face that had deceived her? And now another question occurred. Was it possible that Raven had taken his name as an homage to that Queen's attendant? Hardly likely, but one could never tell with that man.

The gazelle in the garden… the Eton Boating Song… bookshops in Oxford. All very well, but now it struck him that there was no continuity between these snapshots of the infant crawling over the carpet, of the swell at Eton and of the young man he was now. No continuity at all. But memory wanted to provide a plot, for it, like the dream, wanted to tell a story and get published.

CHAPTER THIRTEEEN

Martinmas Term commenced in early October. As Lancelyn stepped off onto the platform at St Andrews Station, he had the strongest sensation that someone or something was waiting for him, perhaps someone with bad news, but certainly no one was waiting for him on the platform. He found a postcard from Marcus on the doormat when he got back to Hepburn Gardens. Marcus had got a second which was good enough for him, since he had no wish to see Oxford ever again. Having settled in with Janet, he had got a job with ITV selling and allocating advertising space. Molly had got a third. There was also a letter informing Lancelyn that his article on Walter de la Mare and Edwardian ghost stories in retrospect had been accepted for publication by *The Times Literary Supplement*. (In that article, after providing a broad Edwardian context, he had concentrated on de la Mare's preoccupation with smallness and how that connected with things on the edge of vision.)

This was the term in which he was to start teaching the special subject on Burton and his *The Anatomy of Melancholy*:

'I hear new news every day, and those ordinary rumours of war, plagues, fires, inundations, thefts, murders, massacres, meteors, comets, spectrums, prodigies, apparitions, of towns taken, cities besieged in France, Germany, Turkey, Persia, Poland, etc, daily musters and preparations, and such-like, which these tempestuous times afford, battles fought, so many men slain, monomachies, shipwrecks, piracies, and sea-fights, peace, leagues, stratagems, and fresh alarums. A confusion of vows, wishes, actions, edicts, petitions, lawsuits, pleas, laws, proclamations, complaints, grievances are daily brought to our ears. New books every day, pamphlets, currantoes, stories, whole catalogues of volumes of all sorts, new paradoxes, opinions, schisms, heresies, controversies in philosophy, religion, etc…'

And there was much more in the same vein. That was how Burton saw it and that was still how it was. Lancelyn read that passage and the listing that continued onto the following page until he had finally internalised its content, before composing himself to lie down once again on the library floor and meditate on the meaning of Burton's book.

Once the immersion had begun, he was startled to find himself in his own library, not only that, but Robert Burton, black pointed beard, black skull cap, flowing black robe and white ruff, was in the room with him and discontentedly scrutinising the books on the shelves. It was indeed an unruly kingdom of paper and it was Burton's opinion that we needed to breed more people, so that the vast number of books here and elsewhere might be read. New books every day. So much was to be pondered upon. *Quot homines, tot sententiae*. Burton suggested that Lancelyn should lie down and make himself comfortable. But Lancelyn was lying down. No, on the sofa over there. Lancelyn had been referred to him as suffering from the love melancholy. What exactly seemed to be the problem? Silence? And more silence? Well perhaps Lancelyn could say something about his dreams. *Et canis in somnis leporis vestigial latrat*: as a dog dreams of a hare, so men dream on such subjects as they thought on last. The dreams which mock us with fleeting shadows are sent neither from the shrines of the gods nor by the gods themselves, but each of us makes his own.

What? Can you still be silent? So be it. It has been said that silence abhors a vacuum and so do I. Then, waving his arm disparagingly at a bookcase, Burton resumed. That which others read of, I feel and practise myself; they get their knowledge from books, I arrive at mine by melancholising. What a glut of books! Who can read them? Surmising that Lancelyn still proposed to add to the number of those books, Burton warned against plagiarising from other books or from quoting excessively from them, since it was a greater offence to steal dead men's writings than their clothes, and too many books were fattened with the compositions of others. They, one and all, whether they were flourishing wits or none such thing, were or would be smothered in oblivion, lie dead and be buried in this our nation. Regarding ingenious puzzles, it was evident that even all our quickest and most flourishing wits, as an owl's eyes at the sun's light waxed dull, were not sufficient to apprehend them, and so much melancholy was provoked by such artificial enigmas. More menacing yet were the kinds and ranks of the nightly witching imps of hell, who had to be conjured out of the thickness of the air and its darkness. When so disturbed and summoned, they necessarily appeared as they had to, just as the Devil had not appeared in Samuel's shape, if only the Witch of Endor had let him alone. The nightly imps then would come on stealthily and insert themselves in a man's depraved humours, and their lascivious provocations molested his fantasy and fanned his intemperate flames of lust. If you have no dreams you shall live within them.

'*Pro captu lectoris, habent sua fata libelli.*' According to the capabilities of the reader, books have their destiny. Yet it may also be the case that, according to the resources of a library, its owner faces his destiny, for some books were too tragical, too much dejecting a man, aggravating offences, and so they brought on melancholy. The devil, who rangeth abroad like a roaring lion, still seeking whom he may devour, in several shapes and dreams entraps deluded human souls. God is the spectator of all miseries. It was certain that they should meet again, for Lancelot's condition necessitated many future appointments, for which a price must be paid. Somehow Burton, though garrulous, had managed to convey all this without speaking any words at all, before sorrowfully shaking his head and departing from their silent session. But it had still left Lancelyn wondering what a curranto was and, more generally, he asked himself what it was that he had learned from his encounter with the incarnation of *The Anatomy of Melancholy*. There was no sofa in the library.

The departmental meeting was held a week before the beginning of term. It opened with more good news. After some teething problems, the new cyclostyle machine was up and running. (But of course, since Lancelyn was suspicious of all technology except motorbikes, he never used the machine.) Then a new external examiner had to be appointed. The university library would need to be provided with lists of all the books reserved for special subjects. The year's new proposals for special subjects were scrutinised. Jaimie was pioneering one on Scottish literature in the age of George Macdonald, whoever he was, and that went through on the nod. But Lancelyn's proposed special subject on Robert Burton's *The Anatomy of Melancholy* and its sources and influences was subjected to heavy criticism by Wormsley, who claimed to be worried that young people ought not to be introduced to the intensive study of madness, since he thought that the students were neurotic enough as it was. But other members of the department, relieved that more of the fourth-year teaching load was being taken on in this fashion, were adamant that Lancelyn's special subject should go ahead. Then Wormsley announced he was worried about the staff's poor record of publication. It reflected badly on the department.

'The only thing that any of us has published recently is Lancelyn's dinky little piece on Walter de la Mare in *The Times Literary Supplement*. I dare say he will soon be joining the metropolitan elite on the strength of it.'

Wormsley had kept the most substantial item till last. This was the establishment of a pilot course in creative writing in the following academic year. He and Jaimie would be running it, but they would welcome the advice and assistance from a couple more members of staff. Neither F.R. Leavis nor C.S. Lewis had been known to be enthusiasts for the teaching of creative writing, and at first Wormsley's appeal met with no response, until Henry protested, 'How can there be academic rigour in a course where any old whimsy has to be taken seriously and where there can be no objective means of assessment? How are students' minds going to be stretched? What new facts will they have learnt? How will this add to the acknowledged body of scholarship? Who will be qualified to take this course, or, come to that, who will *not* be qualified to take it? How is the teacher going to tell a student to his or her face that what he has just been presented with, though it may be heartfelt and very personal, is actually a load of old rubbish without any promise whatsoever? Badly spelled and ungrammatical daydreams will be the almost invariable outcome of such classes. And why should Shakespeare, Johnson, Keats and Conrad be moved over to make space for such a laughably easy option?'

There was a lengthy silence and Lancelyn was enjoying a fantasy in which the young Joseph Conrad was part of a class in creative writing on board the *Judaea* just off Java Head. This would have taken place on the sweltering deck after the regular instruction in the management of the sextant. French and Polish were his first languages and his English would still not have been very good, so he was having difficulty in understanding such matters as the technique of the nautical yarn, delayed decoding and transtextual narrative. Besides this was his first encounter with the real orient and he was squinting in the sun and trying to memorise the sight in the distance of the yellow sand, as well as every other minute detail of the exotic shoreline. But something happened... then to everyone's astonishment, including his own, Lancelyn said that he would very much like to be part of this new creative writing initiative. Wormsley and Jaimie gazed at him first with wonder and then with suspicion. Henry looked aghast. When Lancelyn thought about it later, he realised that he was volunteering in order to learn rather than to teach, because he had *The Prelude* to write and no idea how to set about it. His offer was hesitantly accepted. Once again Sylvie was waiting for Jaimie outside the department and this time she stuck her tongue out at Lancelyn.

Lancelyn and Quentin coincided in the staff common room on the day before term began. Lancelyn had been nervously at work on the crossword. He could not give up on the crossword, but after that sodding séance, he was always nervous that the answer to a particular clue might be something that he was afraid to arrive at. He explained the problem to Quentin.

'Oh, you've got a special case of logophobia.'

Quentin was like a doctor who believed that once the disease had been named, it ceased to be a threat to the patient's health and he was an expert on phobias: chronophobia was fear of the future, lobophobia was fear of women's ear lobes, cacophobia was fear of ugliness, submechanophobia was fear of fully or partially submerged objects, coulrophobia was fear of clowns.

Lancelyn was not reassured by the diagnosis of logophobia and he decided not to confess that he also happened to be a sufferer from chronophobia. So he changed the subject and went on to check with Quentin what ITV was and Quentin explained that there was now a commercial television network. Lancelyn was curious to know how a degree in history qualified one to help sell advertising. He was told that the study of history trained the mind to be critical. Lancelyn wondered what Marcus had to be critical of while he allotted two minutes to an advertisement for toothpaste. Then Quentin also suggested that the study of history enabled the student to make predictions about future economic and cultural trends. Lancelyn replied that, if Edward Gibbon or Lord Macaulay had made useful predictions about future economic and cultural trends, he was not aware of it and he still did not see how this might help sell space for toothpaste commercials. But what Quentin really wanted to talk about was what went on during that séance.

'Perhaps Marcus would acquire the Heinz account. In which case divination via spaghetti could be part of a marketing strategy. Protect your little ones and your hubby from unforeseen dangers by regularly consulting the ancient wisdom of the spaghetti letters. That evening at your place was fun wasn't it? Don't worry about the apparent message of the random spaghetti letters. That is just the sort of thing Bernard and you would pick up. It was an example of pareidolia.'

'What?'

'Pareidolia, the incorrect perception of a pattern or meaning in a chance assemblage of things – like seeing faces in clouds or tree barks, or detecting conspiracies where none exist. By the way, Molly seemed awfully fond of you.'

'We are old friends.'

'Er yes, I could see that. I am guessing that she is sapiosexual.'

'What?' Lancelyn struggled to imagine what this might mean. Was it possible that Molly was sexually attracted by half-submerged objects? Or that she only did it with clowns?

Or, more banally, she just liked feeling for men's penises?'

'Molly is obviously sexually attracted by intelligence.'

'I see… and is there a word for being sexually attracted to stupidity?'

'Of, course. Morophilia.'

Morophilia. Morophilia. Morophilia. Commit it to memory. One never knew when that word might come in handy. Now Jaimie joined them. They wanted to know how his novel was getting on, and they learnt that it was getting on famously. His imagination has been set free by setting his story in old Shanghai. It is about a young Scottish tycoon with a passion for reading Robert Burns and walking the hills and mountains around Shanghai. On one of these walks in the tropical gloaming he encounters a beautiful young blonde punting a sampan across one of the local lakes. He invites her and her husband to a Burns Night in the city. That was as far as he had got.

Quentin was enthusiastic, 'This could be a big hit, like *The World of Suzie Wong* but with a bonny Scottish lassie.'

Jaimie looked baffled, but Quentin promised to lend him a copy of the novel.

Jaimie had recently sat in on that Edinburgh conference on ghost stories. Apparently it had given Bernard, as one of the convenors and opening speakers, an opportunity to promote his imminently forthcoming book, *Towards a Reinvention of Edwardian Fictionality: Deconstructing the Hegemonic Ghost Stories of M.R. James*. Obviously Bernard had dropped the P.G. Wodehouse angle. 'Reinvention' sounded pretty serious. These days reinvention was a big thing in literary studies. Presumably those who used the term had borrowed it from the scientists and scientists also spent a lot of time reinventing things. Once Lancelyn got back to Hepburn Gardens he wrote to the editor of the *TLS* asking if he could review Bernard's book when it was published.

CHAPTER FOURTEEN

Though he had hoped to get ideas from Raven regarding the composition of *The Prelude*, in his heart he knew that his time with a guru was past and that he would have to learn to be his own master. Youth! He remembered Henry quoting Conrad to him: 'And this is all that is left of it! Only a moment of strength, of romance, of glamour, of youth.' To fix youth in writing was like pinning a butterfly to a wheel. And how could he write about youth without imitating the way old people did it? At the end of it all, so what? Why would anyone want to publish his stuff? More immediately important, what could there be in *The Prelude* to suggest to Molly that these surely rather ordinary scraps of memory were indeed the foreshadowing of something tremendous? After all, what had he done, except read many books and later do a lot of rowing as well? But then, come to think of it, what had Proust done before he wrote his masterpiece? He was not exactly a man of action, was he? Nevertheless Lancelyn had to find a way of engineering his narrative in such a way as to suggest that his whole short life up to this point had been but a prelude to his encounter with Molly and that she was the Expected One, the woman prefigured in his dreams, and once united, they would do such things... as what? And then, how should Bernard feature in the book, if at all?

Faced with such imponderable questions, it was a relief in the first week of term to turn to the first meeting of the special subject, 'Robert Burton's *The Anatomy of Melancholy* (1621), Its Sources and Influences'. He had a decent take-up of fifteen students, quite a few of whom were pretty girls. He began by talking about the title of Burton's book, the full version of which was *The Anatomy of Melancholy, What it is; With All the Kinds, Causes, Symptomes, Prognostickes, and Several Cures of it. In Three Maine Partitions with their several Sections, Members, and Subsections. Philosophically, Historically, Opened and Cut up.* Then he gave a thumbnail sketch of the man's life and followed this up with an example of Burton's investigations into the causes of melancholy. Cabbage was the example that Lancelyn chose. 'It causeth troublesome dreams, and sends up black vapours to the brain. Galen... of all herbs condemns cabbage; and Isaac... it brings heaviness to the soul.' This led on to a mini-lecture on the second-century Greek physician Galen and his belief that disease was caused by an imbalance between the four humours, blood, phlegm, yellow bile and black bile. Cabbage produced black bile which, according to Galen, was secreted in the spleen. The word 'melancholia' was derived from the Greek for black bile. Watery cabbage was a

165

disgusting and dangerous thing.

But a little later, registering the students' looks of dismay as they were confronted with the sheer logorrheic bulk of what Burton had produced, Lancelyn spent the second half of the session giving his class a crash course in the elements of speed reading. Despite Wormsley's fears about depressed students getting yet more depressed as they plumbed the depths of the literary melancholy of the seventeenth century, there was lots of laughter in the class. He brought it to an end by announcing that he was suffering from love melancholy and that was what they should read about in preparation for the next meeting. Some of the girls sighed.

A few days' later *Towards a Reinvention of Edwardian Fictionality* arrived.

Bernard's introduction began as follows:

As Roland Barthes has reminded us in *Le Degré zero de l'écriture*, the language of literature is peculiarly imbricated in modernity and its discursive orders. In what follows I have sought to challengingly situate the stories of M.R. James within a time-bound hegemonic structure and to demonstrate how in his works and those of his contemporaries the fictive concept of the 'ghost' was deployed and then to subject this deployment to an analysis which inevitably will draw on Antonio Gramsci's understanding of how social and economic forces constrain and deform cultural forms. With this necessarily politicised programme in mind, I have sought to interrogate the ghost stories of James and critique their class-ridden, imperialist and sexist subtexts, and further to also analytically interrogate the bad faith that underlies those texts. The problem of the pleasure that readers of such stories are alleged to have experienced must of necessity raise further questions regarding *jouissance* and bad faith on the part of the readership. James' metaphorical and metonymic devices are here decoded and, in the light of Jacques Lacan's compelling insights, attention is drawn to ways in which the author's intentions have been subverted by signifiers of absence and difference. Naturally, this undertaking is merely an exploratory interrogation of a territory which has up to this point in time been strangely neglected and consequently many questions have been left unanswered, but asking the questions hopefully is more valuable than any answers that I might have been able to give.

Bernard's introduction continued by telling its readers in some detail exactly what the book was going to say in its following chapters. While this removed any possibility of surprise in reading what was to come, for Lancelyn this was a mercy, since he did not care much for surprise and excitement. Still, he wondered if it was worth his time reading the rest of the book before writing his review. The introduction concluded with effusive thanks to Molly, his 'helpmeet'. In the end Lancelyn decided that it would be sufficient to skim the rest of the book.

Chapter one dealt with class issues. The author and his stories were the product of an Eton and Oxbridge upbringing and they unconsciously revealed the consequent self-entitlement that led James to patronise both his characters and his readers. Yokels and servants were there, often as not, for comic effect. They were not reliable witnesses of supernatural manifestations. Those were reserved for gentlemen of a scholarly turn of mind. Moreover the manifestations preferred to manifest themselves in rather grand houses. Ghost stories were deployed to strengthen the class system and patriarchy. More on patriarchy was promised in the third chapter.

Chapter two dealt with the latent subtext of imperialism in the stories. To the unskilled reader imperialism was conspicuous by its absence in the stories, but it could be seen that it was precisely this conspicuous absence that was relevant and important. Bernard drew attention to the ring in 'Oh, Whistle, and I'll Come to You, My Lad' with its inscription 'Who is this, who is coming?' which plays such a large part in the haunting of Professor Parkins. The ring, which by its nature must be constructed around a hole, which is to say an absence, could be seen as an unmistakable metaphor for imperialism and its ill-gotten riches, which was the telling absence in this story and the others. The big houses and the harmlessly antiquarian old England, which were so often the preferred haunts of ghosts, surely owed a great deal, perhaps everything, to the profits of imperialism and the labours of those toiling in sugarcane plantations in the Caribbean or sweatshops in India and yet James was careful to elide the vital economic background to the ghostly manifestations of evil that he had conjured up. Thus the insubstantial supernatural could be seen as a device for concealing the real evils of economic oppression.

The third chapter explored the sexuality which was palpable in the stories and concealed in James' own life. Formally there was no sex in the ghost stories, but of course,

James' behaviour and his stories alike betrayed clear signs of misogyny and closet homosexuality. In the Jamesian imagination the 'wet lips' that whispered in the ear of Dr Haynes in 'The Stalls of Barchester Cathedral' were as clear a signifier of the author's deplorable bad faith, as in quite another context, the kiss of Judas was. In the patriarchal world of James, men are the privileged recipients of hauntings and for example the maid's task in 'Oh, Whistle, and I'll Come to You, My Lad' is merely to make up the spare bed after its sheets have been all crumpled from the ghostly visitant having slept in that bed. Attention might also be drawn to the moth with teeth in 'Casting the Runes' which it could be argued was a vagina dentata. It could further be argued that there was a sense in which M.R. James, imperialist, sexist and a snob, was more truly sinister than any of his creations. Bernard concluded by calling for a further, more generally politicised re-evaluation of the ghost story.

The publisher's blurb assured the prospective buyer that this insightful volume was the definitive analysis of the ghost story.

Lancelyn hesitated before beginning his review. Suppose Bernard was right after all? But no, dammit. While he was not entirely sure that he understood what Bernard was on about, with all those polysyllables and dropped foreign names helping to obscure his meaning, he was mostly pretty sure that he did not care for it and he sensed that he – Eton and Oxbridge, scholarly and scared of women – was the book's real target, not M.R. James. In any case, their friendship was over. It was perhaps like the final scene in *The House on Pooh Corner* where Christopher Robin says goodbye to his bear, though Lancelyn could not decide whether he was Christopher Robin or Pooh. Besides, he told himself that it might be doing Bernard a kindness to point out what was wrong with the book and then he would be grateful. Well, that was remotely possible. No, it was not. Anyway he did not want Bernard to be grateful. Bernard still had Molly, an All Soul's fellowship and a book out. Why should he have everything? Then again, it was quite possible that Bernard would not succeed in guessing who had written the anonymous review.

Lancelyn began his review by confessing that since he was an unskilled reader, he had not hitherto spotted the conspicuous quality of the absence of imperialism in these ghost stories, but then he had not spotted it in *The Teddy Bear Coalman's Picnic*, *Middlemarch* or the Jeeves and Wooster stories either. It was of course refreshing to find a fellow of All Souls so concerned about the proletariat and the way they were being cheated out of their share of spectral visions. Misogynists and homosexuals should be warned that if they were tempted to turn to stories like *The Stalls of Barchester Cathedral* for easy gratification of their sexual preferences, they would find very slim pickings indeed. Taken as a whole, the book was a lazy polemic against past ways of doing and seeing things, and the past, being past, could not answer back.

But the most original feature of this otherwise tediously pretentious book was the author's decision to present Karswell, the sinister scholar, sorcerer and evil protagonist of 'Casting the Runes', as the most truly admirable of all James' creations, for according to *Towards a Reinvention of Edwardian Fictionality*, Karswell was a rebel against stuffy academic traditions and antiquarian pseudo-scholarship. Since he was opposed to the establishment, he was on the side of the angels. (The dark angels?) Towards the end of the review Lancelyn borrowed a line from James' 'Casting the Runes', in order to characterise Bernard's book as being 'written in no sort of style at all – split infinitives, and every sort of thing that makes an Oxford gorge rise'. As for the publisher's blurb, the book was perhaps 'definitive' in that it was likely to kill any future interest in the subject.

Back to *The Prelude*, which in reality was to be written for one person and one person alone. The broader reading public could follow on behind. It was obviously going to be necessary to remodel his past in order to give it the narrative unity which it did not possess, but which it deserved. He went back to the beginning and that carpet in Teheran. This time the determined and drooling infant, who patiently crawled backwards and forwards over it, discovered something that he was far from able to put words to. One cloudy and humid afternoon he was for the first time successful in tracing the figure in the carpet, and as he did so, this revelation imposed a pattern on his life, though in some baffling way his discovery had already been part of that pattern. The baby had a vision, an abstract vision, of what the carpet-weaver could not possibly have been aware, which was the mystery of the man that the baby was to become. In retrospect, finding the figure in the carpet was perhaps a little like reading one's own palm and discovering for the first time one's lifeline and mount of Venus.

That should make his infancy a bit more interesting. The next thing to do was to beef up his schoolboy meeting with Iron Foot Jack. There was no need to hurry Jack out of the coffee house. The film people could wait and he and Jack could have a longer talk. So there Jack was and he was saying, 'If you summon me, no matter when and no matter what the circumstances, put out the word for me and I'll come to you. And the reason why? Cos you're like I am, a prince. You've the physiog of a prince of two worlds. Adam and Eve me. 'Ell is built of yuman souls. A man who 'as died does not know that he's pushing up the daisies and he thinks 'e is at 'ome, for there are two Lunnon Tahns, very alike, but one earthy, the other deathly and, sooner or later, 'e will meet with a demon or an angel. If it's a demon 'e can kiss his physiog goodbye, for the damned are faceless, and the demons, being learned, speak only in Latin. So that's 'ard. It's all in *'Eaven an' its Wonders an' Ell* by a cove called Swedenborg. I dare say you'll come to 'im by and by. You'll need his 'elp in the ordeal that's comin' your way. There'll be a 'orrid fat ass, but your princely self will come through and waiting for you will be a bit of alright in the way of an angelic good-looker with knockers like melons and a Khyber Pass to die for an' she'll be yours forever. Your cows an' kisses.'

Lancelyn wrote that only later did he realise that 'fat ass' was Cockney rhyming slang for black mass, whereas 'Khyber Pass' meant arse and 'cows and kisses' meant Mrs. Then, having written up the early episodes, he realised that he needed to know a bit about black magic. He asked Quentin for help.

'Oh good. By all means. I hope this is going to lead on to another séance… or better yet, a satanic ritual. This place could do with some livening up. The only thing I have got is a couple of novels by a man called Dennis Wheatley, but he seemed pretty knowledgeable about the subject and writing from experience. He is rumoured to have been a friend of Aleister Crowley.'

The following lunchtime Quentin produced copies of *The Devil Rides Out* and *To the Devil a Daughter* and he read out loud from Wheatley's opening note to *The Devil Rides Out*: 'Should any of my readers incline to a serious study of the subject, and thus come in contact with a man or woman of Power, I feel that it is only right to urge them, most strongly to refrain from being drawn into the practice of the Secret Art in any way. My own observations have led me to an absolute conviction that to do so would bring them into dangers of a very real and concrete nature.'

Good. The novels were convincingly sinister. This was exactly the sort of stuff that Lancelyn was looking for and he was now ready to produce an embellished account of his time in Oxford with Bernard. Except there was of course the possibility of a case for libel. So Bernard would have to become Bertrand and Molly Anne. Also Bertrand would be reading French, not English, and he would be at Magdalen, not Merton. Then Lancelyn roughed out some bread-and-butter stuff about their meeting at the freshman's fair, idyllic days punting on the Isis and no less idyllic evenings toasting crumpets and talking about the meaning of life. There was only one armchair in Bertrand's rooms and it was occupied by an enormous teddy bear called Bilbo. So they usually sat on the floor. Bertrand, charismatic and witty, was quite a swell in his velvet corduroy jacket and foulard scarf. He was, as he invariably said, 'very much as ever, "burning with a hard gem-like flame"', and always up for a bit of roistering. And he was clever too. He was, as he boasted, 'the sort of fellow who eats lots of fish'. In his third year he attracted the affections of an undergraduette called Anne who was perhaps the most beautiful student of her day. Though Lancelyn had loved her grace and elegance, it was from an honourable distance. A golden and untainted future seemed to beckon to Bertrand and Anne and Lancelyn was glad for them.

When a thing is complete, it begins to fall apart. Bertrand, brilliant though he was, started to worry about finals. He also began to avoid Lancelyn, whose first thought was that it might be Anne who was taking his best friend away from him, though this was not so. On the rare occasions that he coincided with Bertrand in libraries, some of the books Bertrand was reading seemed rather strange, and Bertrand, who by now had turned unfriendly, took to calling him 'Bilbo'. Then one Sunday afternoon Lancelyn decided to visit him in his room in Magdalen. Though Bertrand's room was unlocked, he was not there. Lancelyn took one look round and then what he had seen made him retreat and close the door. Though Bilbo was in his accustomed armchair, he was now covered in pins and there was a noose around his neck.

Lancelyn wrote that afterwards it took him many months to piece together what had been going on during Bertrand's final terms in Oxford. Bertrand, feeling he needed more than ordinary help as he approached finals, had come across the novels of Dennis Wheatley and then went on to consult other more practical treatises on the black arts, as he sought to conjure up spirits who could increase his intelligence, tell him in advance what questions would come up in the final exams and transform Anne from a loving companion into his sexual slave. Then, when he came across Dennis Wheatley's novel, *The Devil Rides Out*, he was favourably struck by the character of the book's leading villain, the satanic Mr Damien

Mocata. It was rather odd that Bertrand should go on to choose Mocata as his role model, since at first sight Mocata was unprepossessing: 'a pot-bellied, bald-headed man of about sixty, with large, protuberant, fishy eyes, limp hands, and most unattractive lisp'. But Mocata, a rebel against the Anglo-Saxon establishment, despised conventions, and more than that, he was a Man of Knowledge. Though he walked in the sunshine he had no shadow. According to Mocata, 'In magic, there is neither good nor evil. It is only the science of causing change to occur by means of the will.' Following the starting guidelines that Wheatley had cautiously alluded to in the novel, Bertrand was successful in summoning up certain entities, or at least in believing that he had, and it seemed to him that these entities assisted him in gaining his starred first. A fellowship at Cambridge followed almost immediately and it was not long before he published his first book, *The Devil Takes Care of His Own: Paradox and Paradigm in the Popular Fictions of Dennis Wheatley*. According to its blurb, this was 'a ground-breaking critique of the function of normative "shocker fiction" and its postulates of ritual substitutability'. Lancelyn described how he had glanced at the book and found that Bertrand's text was peppered with invocations to strangely spelt foreign names that might have been those of demons. He could make little of the book, which was savagely and anonymously reviewed in *The Times Literary Supplement* by a senior bishop. Of course Lancelyn also worried about Anne and he imagined her splayed out naked on an altar in front of Bertrand who was wearing only a black mask and an apron. He imagined that quite a lot. So far so good. As so often in life, the imaginary friend seemed more interesting than the one that had been offered by reality.

He was enjoying this. But then he had to stop. How could he possibly write about his night with Molly in St Andrews? And why would the sinister Bertrand be visiting him in St Andrews, unless… unless he had agreed to Anne's desire to visit Lancelyn in St Andrews, because this would give him the opportunity to plant some sort of curse in Lancelyn's house. If Bertrand had been an expert devotee of M.R. James, it would have been a piece of paper inscribed with cursed runic letters, but Bertrand would have to work his evil with something more Wheatleyesque. Let it be the mummified penis of the evil high priest, Seth. Then Bertrand arranges to be invited to St Andrews by the unsuspecting Lancelyn. So Bertrand, Anne and the penis of Seth turn up in St Andrews. She is looking particularly glamorous in her big floppy hat, but Lancelyn could see that she was afraid of something. She will want his help, but she will be afraid to leave Bertrand. What now? How can he possibly defeat Bertrand and rescue Anne? Even more difficult, how could he explain and describe that night of rapture in bed?

He had found the fantasy most enjoyable. But then he felt qualms. Suppose it was not entirely fantasy. Suppose that Bernard had been ready to agree to Molly's wish to visit Lancelyn in Scotland because this would give this devotee of Karswell the chance to plant maleficent runes somewhere in the house in Hepburn Gardens. Of course that was ridiculous. Of course. But it would explain why Lancelyn felt mysteriously threatened whenever he returned to his house. Then, come to think of it, that morning when they went for the walk on the West Sands, just before the walk, he had walked in on

Bernard in the library and Bernard seemed to be examining a book which he hastily put back on the shelf. Had he slipped something inside the book? This was absurd. He must be going mad. But, mad or not, he would search the relevant shelves. If the runes had been planted there, then they were a ticking time-bomb. Every book in the vicinity of where Bernard has been standing would have to be taken off the shelves and its pages flicked through. Any bookmarks he might discover should be destroyed. Also, where necessary, the gap between the binding and the sewed pages should be scrutinised. Or there might be a razor-thin slit in one of the leather bindings. Then it was possible that the runes were working their evil from behind a bogus bookplate. Further composition of *The Prelude* had to be put aside and Lancelyn's search took hours. He found nothing, and though this should have calmed him, it did not. The sense of oppression and the menace was still with him, and if anything, it was stronger than ever. It was autumn and outside the house the dark was coming on rapidly.

The next day was the second meeting of the special subject on *The Anatomy of Melancholy* and they would be looking at what passed for the scientific study of desire in the seventeenth century. Lancelyn found it a strange experience to be formally instructing a class in the nature of the ailment which he was suffering from. They were all young and he was hardly much older than they were, and as Burton put it, 'youth is *benigna in amorem, et prona materies*, a very combustible matter, naphtha itself, the fuel of love's fire, and most apt to kindle it'. Yet though love might be a painful ailment, reading, the right sort of reading, might be the cure, since for Burton, reading was a kind of medicine, or even a dynamic form of magic. Just as certain alchemists had taught that the reader did not have to actually carry out the experiments described in books, since to read about them would be sufficient to achieve the alchemical enlightenment that was obscurely promised. Yet, though Lancelyn felt sick with desire for Molly, it was a sickness that he did not wish to be cured from.

From love melancholy, they eventually moved in later classes on to religious melancholy which Burton regarded as a special type of love melancholy. So much melancholy. The class wanted to know if Burton was a cheerful sort of bloke. A good question. From what Lancelyn had seen of the man in his library, Burton was not the sort of bloke to share a convivial pint with. Moreover, in his *Brief Lives,* John Aubrey reported that Burton hanged himself and, according to others, he chose the date of his suicide to fit the day predicted for his death by his horoscope. But Lancelyn told the class that when Burton was feeling depressed he would go out to Magdalen Bridge and swear at the boatmen passing beneath, before returning to his rooms greatly cheered.

The students complained about the amount of Latin in *The Anatomy of Melancholy.* Lancelyn told them to ignore the Latin tags. That was just Burton's scholarly swank. But a little later he was telling them about an exciting new book, *Folie et Déraison: Histoire de la folie à l'age classique* by Michel Foucault, but when he checked how many of them had a reading knowledge of French, only two girls put up their hands. So he had to spoon feed them the author's romantically panoramic history of madness from the medieval Ship of Fools to the Renaissance invention of female hysteria to the seventeenth-century Great Confinement and beyond.

CHAPTER FIFTEEN

The Creative Writing Working Party, all three of them, met in Wormsley's office. Prints of illustrations by Rackham, Tenniel and Pauline Baynes were on the walls. They gave the room the feel of a kindergarten, an impression which the presence of a stuffed lion in the corner did nothing to dispel. There was also an enormous railway map of Great Britain on one of the walls. The meeting began with Wormsley fulminating about Henry and his intervention at the departmental meeting and how the man was really a living fossil, incapable of understanding the modern world that he found himself in. There was a sense in which that man had actually died on one of Dieppe's beaches and what was left of him was incapable of recognising the vast possibilities that would be opened up by a creative writing course. Then Wormsley rounded on Lancelyn. What was he doing at this meeting, since he only taught non-fiction? And besides there were no novels in the seventeenth century. There was no need to be polite, so Lancelyn told Wormsley that he was surprised to find him so ignorant. What about *Don Quixote*, *Oroonoko*, *The Pilgrim's Progress*, *La Princesse de Clèves* and *Simplicissimus*? There were also plenty of seventeenth-century poets. Moreover, as it happened, he was proposing to devote a meeting of his special subject class to the influence of *The Anatomy of Melancholy* on *Tristram Shandy*. Wormsley then said that, if Lancelyn had turned up at this meeting in the hope of currying favour with him, then he was deluded, but he was glad to hear that he still had a sharp tongue in his head.

It was time to move on to drafting the advertisement for the course:

> Do you enjoy reading?
> Why only read other people's books?
> Why not write your own?

Publishers are always desperately looking for books, stories and poems to publish. Satisfying their need will be very profitable as well as lots of fun. Unlock the creative you. In this vibrant university-level course, instruction will be given in narrative, plot, characterisation and style, and as you master these things, your imagination will be set free and you will find your own voice. Originality has its rules and it can be learnt and we are in the business of teaching originality. Our expert guidance will give you faith not only in who you are, but how to express who you are. The road to publication can be a long one and there may be obstacles on the way, but there is no need to set out on this exciting journey alone. Why not travel in the company of like-minded creative people in the historic and picturesque town of St Andrews? We are here, waiting to teach you the rules of being imaginatively creative and kick-start your career as a real author.

They agreed that the critical reading of a selection of published works should supplement all the stuff about time-frames, narrative voice and what not. Wormsley favoured the novels of C.S. Lewis. Jaimie suggested Sir Walter Scott, though Richard Mason's *The World of Suzie Wong* had made quite an impression on him. The James Bond novels were Lancelyn's choice. Then they needed a famous published name as a guest to front the course. Muriel Spark was up and coming. Would she do? Then how was the teaching load to be distributed? And where were the advertisements to be placed? Wormsley wanted to bring in a psychologist from Dundee, though he did not explain why.

All these things would have to be decided at their next meeting. Wormsley told them that the Master was keen on this project since it would give the university a more transatlantic, go-ahead feel. Finally it would help if Lancelyn could publish something more substantial on Walter de la Mare.

Four weeks later the review of *Towards a Reinvention of Edwardian Fictionality* was published and Lancelyn opened a bottle of champagne, but then, as he stared down into his glass, he realised that the waiting period had now begun. Where would the axe fall? How would it fall? Would Bernard confine himself to a stiff letter to the *TLS*? Or would he hire a couple of thugs to beat him up? Or could he take it out on Molly? Or following Karswell's example, might he seek to put a magical curse upon him? But then would Bernard spot who had written the review? And would someone show it to Molly? What would she think?

The next time he was in the common room, Quentin waved the *TLS* at him.

'Your friend Bernard has had a rotten review here.' The raised eyebrow suggested that he was about to say something more, but at that point Henry joined them and Quentin showed him the review. Henry read it carefully and smiled sadly before commenting, 'Yes, it is quite funny, but surely, since we live in a cruel world, there is no need to make it yet crueller. Think how hard this poor man will have laboured to produce this book, only to see it cursorily summarised and then mocked by a reviewer who operates behind the nasty mask of anonymity. However much a reviewer may disagree with what he is reviewing, he should always be courteous, and scholarly study should not be turned into a gladiatorial arena.

If one cannot find anything nice to say about a book, why say anything at all? But never mind all that. Whatever possessed you, Lancelyn, to volunteer for this abomination called a creative writing course?'

Lancelyn had been busy, pretending to fish around for his cigarettes. He replied, 'You must look upon me as your spy and keep it under your hat, but I thought someone ought to keep an eye on what Wormsley is up to. There is something fishy about his proposal. I don't think that it is quite what it seems.'

'You are hinting that it may be something quite exciting,' 0s1aid Quentin. 'A front for gun-running? Witchcraft? White slavery? A Neo-Nazi indoctrination course?'

'Knowing Wormsley, I wouldn't put that last one past him,'

said Henry. 'Ah well. How did you find today's crossword?'

'Er, I got three clues.'

'One more than me. Some days it just seems that the clues have been set by an alien mind.'

Thereupon they fell to speculating that every now and again the editor of *The Times* invited a Martian to be the setter of the day's crossword. From there they drifted on to discussing how during the war, the decoding outfit at Bletchley Park had taken as some of their recruits the fastest solvers of a certain crossword and how odd it was that the crossword in question was a *Daily Telegraph* one.

'*The Telegraph* crossword is always a doddle,' said Henry. 'If only I had seen it, I might have avoided the Dieppe landing and spent the rest of the war years contentedly solving *Telegraph*-standard puzzles in Bletchley.'

Then Quentin suggested that Lancelyn should write a letter to the *TLS* in defence of his friend's book. Just for a few seconds this seemed like a good idea and Lancelyn was starting to think about how to phrase it when he realised that the editor of the *TLS* would think that he was a raving lunatic, writing in to denounce his own review.

At last a letter from Molly arrived:

Darling Lancelyn,

As I write this I am looking out of the kitchen window at our dilapidated garden. The stone walkway is getting overgrown, the fencing and gateposts are sagging and a solitary magpie sits on the branch of a sycamore tree that has already lost all its leaves. So I do not need to describe how I am feeling. What can be seen outside my kitchen window says it all. We have rented a small house in Headington. Darling, you are so far away and yet you feel so close, as if you were with me looking out of the window. How is *The Prelude* going? Part of me wants to say 'hurry up', but the better part of me says, 'Don't hurry up.' You need to make it as good as you can. But still 'hurry up', because I want the two of us to be together again as soon as possible. It is no fun being an academic wife. I hope you are not going to be a lecturer forever. We always seem to be strapped for cash and Bernard is a bit strange these days, moody and prone to sudden fits of rage. He never laughs or sings and he eats in college whenever he can. His book has apparently had a sneery review in *The Times Literary Supplement*. I had lunch with Raven last week and he told me that he is sure he knows who wrote the review, but he will not say. Bernard is fairly confident that it must be one of his All Souls colleagues and says that they are all fuddy-duddy, old farts. He and they are not getting on and I think he is worried that his fellowship will not be continued, but he will not talk about it. He does not know what to do now. He talks about following up on some French intellectual's insights with a book on what he calls 'the death of the reader', but he does not seem to be getting very far with it. Here I am writing about Bernard and not about me, but what have I got to write about? Being an academic wife is not what I was born for. I think of you all the time and long to know how you are. But do not write to me, since that might be dangerous.

We must meet in London. Do not write to me, but let us meet in Le Macabre when your term ends. I will send you a note to tell you when. Be patient (as I must be). I know that I am asking a lot of you, but I have to know that you deserve my love.

For the time being you have my love, whether deserved or not, Molly

Was he in love with Molly? Perhaps he should define his terms. What was love? That was hard to pin down exactly, since 176, was lust, sex and reproduction, 177, was the ethics of social relations, and 177.7,0. was loving relationships, all within the realm of philosophy and psychology. On the other hand the sociology of dating was 306.73, a long way from the 170s. And then 'women' was of course part of etiquette in the 390s. The taxonomy of love made no sense.

In the weeks that followed Molly's letter he continued to work on *The Prelude* in a surely doomed attempt to present his life so far as marked by unmistakable signs of his coming greatness. He dipped into *Mein Kampf* for tips on how to do this, but Hitler offered his readers only struggle, danger and death, and Lancelyn did not want this to be his promise to Molly. Finally he could do no more with what he had written. Molly gave him a date for their meeting in Le Macabre. In the intervening weeks Lancelyn managed to put together another article about Walter de la Mare, this time about de la Mare's scrupulous avoidance in horror stories such as 'Seaton's Aunt', 'Out of the Deep' and 'All Hallows' of climaxes or conclusions that needed to be spelt out. Whereas M.R. James' apparitions and monsters were all too tangible, those of de la Mare remained in the shadows and perhaps they were not there at all. He sent this off to *Encounter* was pleased to learn by return of post that it had been accepted for publication.

CHAPTER SIXTEEN

It was an enormous relief to be back in London, even if the craving to buy more books was stronger than ever. Increasingly he found booksellers very tiresome. They would ask him what he was looking for – to which his only answer could be that he was looking for a book that he did not know existed. Only when he had found it would he know that it was exactly this book that he had been seeking. This time he failed to find any non-existent books, though he was pleased to acquire a most useful biography of Robert Burton, *Hellebore and Borage*, as well as a life of Melvin Dewey and a copy of *Geophagy during Pregnancy in Africa*. The last would fill a definite gap in his library. Then he proceeded on to Le Macabre. She was there before him and they hugged.

'I am supposed to be shopping,' she said, 'but with the allowance he gives me I don't know what I can shop for.'

He bought Molly her second coffee and put 'The Dead March' from *Saul* on the jukebox. When he told her that it was their tune she smiled sadly. Then he pushed a thick envelope containing a carbon copy of what there was of *The Prelude* towards her, 'This is as much as I have been able to write. You have to decide how our story ends. What do we do now? I wish we had someone to make the decision for us.'

She sighed before replying, 'Remember how we three marched out from here singing? We had no problems then. Bernard never sings now. That review in *The Times Literary Supplement* was even more damaging than he at first thought and he is frightened that his fellowship may not be renewed. And you? You don't look as though you are ready for a singsong either. You look like a haunted man.'

Lancelyn told her that this might not be so far from the truth. He told her about his ridiculous fantasy that Bernard had become obsessed with M.R. James' fictional alchemist Karswell and that he had only accompanied Molly to St Andrews so that he might plant maleficent, perhaps even deadly, runes upon him. Of course it was ridiculous...

Molly agreed, 'You are right! It is absolutely fucking ridiculous! I have never heard of such a thing as death-dealing runes. More to the point, Bernard is no kind of sorcerer. I even wish he were. That would make him a more interesting man than the one he has become. You should know that he does not believe in ghosts, magic or ancient curses. According to him, they are social constructs or something. It is you who are obsessed with magic. And besides Bernard still likes you.'

'He does?'

'Of course he does. And he admires you. He liked the

article you wrote on Walter de la Mare in *The Times Literary Supplement*. He had thought that you had completely given up on ghost stories when you switched to seventeenth-century literature.'

Lancelyn sat in silent thought for a while. Then, 'Alright. I agree that it does seem a bit absurd that he should come up to St Andrews in order to put a curse on me, before giving you his blessing for us sleeping together. What was going on then?'

'I told him that either he came with me, or I went up with Marcus and Janet, but without him, and if Marcus and Janet were to ask, I would explain what I was planning to do. I think that he is almost as scared of me as you bloody are.'

'But then why did you go back to him?'

'I had to be fair. On the train back to London I told him that I was also giving him a chance to prove himself worthy of me. But he should know that it was not my life's ambition to be the woman who inspired some ratty old academic thesis. My beauty must have a purpose.'

'Are we the only two horses in this race? And is he writing a memoir too?'

Then Molly began to cry noisily and other people in the coffee bar were looking round at them. Albinoni's Adagio Celebre was playing on the jukebox.

'This is all such a fucking mess,' she said when she was able to speak. 'You are so far away, and I don't just mean living in Scotland. And Bernard... he... Raven says that his academic career is just about finished.'

Hearing this, Lancelyn fancied that with his little review he had become Shiva, 'The Destroyer of Worlds'. But Molly would surely be outraged and disgusted if she learnt that he had written that piece. She must never ever guess. Surely Raven could not know for sure who had written it?

'He should not let a bad review get him down so much.'

'It is not that the review is hostile. It is that he fears that it may be accurate. But here we are talking about Bernard when we should be talking about us.'

It was a mercy that Molly, with her face buried in her handkerchief, was not looking at him. She continued, 'All the same, Raven is delighted. He thinks that you and Bernard are far too clever to be academics. Teaching is the waste of a good brain. Besides, he says that Bernard's soul is far more important than his career, and spiritual poverty will be good for him. Recently, whenever we have lunch together, Raven has been trying to recruit me as one of his apostles, but his mind keeps wandering off and then he starts talking about how he is looking forward to his retirement. He has taken to calling me Lillith. I don't know why.'

'Maybe he is thinking of "Lillith", a sonnet by Dante Gabriel Rossetti,' and Lancelyn recited:

'And still she sits, young while the earth is old,
  And, subtly of herself contemplative,
  Draws men to watch the bright web she can weave.'

'That makes me sound like some kind of spider,' said Molly, 'but I feel more like the fly that has been trapped by the spider. It is true though that Raven keeps muttering mysteriously about a pattern that is being made.'

Then they sat in silence for a while, smoked and listened to the music. The dancing skeletons on the walls seemed inappropriately cheerful. Finally, Lancelyn said, 'Come back with me now. You don't love him.'

'I don't not love him. Besides he is so sad. I think he needs me more than you do.'

Molly was still in tears when she left Le Macabre. After she had gone, Lancelyn sat down on the pavement outside. It was raining. He too would have liked to have wept, but 'blubbing' had been forbidden at Eton, and since then this ordinary human response had become physically impossible for him. He wondered if he should travel up to Oxford and seek some sort of absolution from Raven. But no. Anyway, it was unlikely that Raven had correctly worked out who had written the review. Now he would have to return to *The Prelude*, a confection of falsehoods that was already beginning to sicken him. Whether he would be the villain of his own story, or whether that station would be held by anyone else, its pages must show. What would Molly make of *The Prelude*? How long must he wait before she came to him? He had read somewhere that beauty was the promise of happiness, but could that possibly be true? Raven had predicted a broken heart. For an instant back then in the coffee bar Lancelyn had fancied himself as Shiva the Destroyer, but the awful thought came to him that he might after all more closely resemble the vengeful Karswell. He wished he had never read that story. Perhaps these sort of narratives were driving him mad. Never mind Raven. Perhaps it was Bernard that he should seek absolution from. Impossible. Though Lancelyn thought of himself as an imaginative sort of person, he could not imagine himself doing that. Never.

Now he had no tears, but when he looked back on how

often he had been found crying in his early years at that school and how he had been beaten and bullied out of it, he started to wonder about the way his memories had been following on behind him, mopping up early disasters and sorrows and in their stead conjuring up a boy's paradise. Compulsory fagging, compulsory chapel, compulsory Officers' Training Corps, punishment runs, cold showers, ceremonially conducted floggings and furtive masturbation. If it had been a paradise, it had certainly been a poisoned one. He had spent most of his time hiding from other boys and reading. Only his last two years had been tolerable and only in his last year had he been elected to Pop, on the strength of his rowing and his precocious erudition, but mostly the rowing. So memory was a compulsive liar and in ten or twenty years' time what lies would it be telling him about his meeting with Molly today?

CHAPTER SEVENTEEN

Spring was slow to arrive in Scotland. Once back in St Andrews with his literary spoils, he immediately set about shelving them, though there was very little space left for new acquisitions. Then, as he tried to find a place for the biography of Dewey, he found that he already had a copy of this book. That kind of thing kept happening. It was time, it was more than time that he set about re-shelving his books and reorganising them according to the Dewey Decimal System. He felt sick to his stomach at the thought of all the labour involved and the dust that would go everywhere.

Some bits of the decimal range would be overcrowded, as his collection was in a sense malformed. It was a monster with some parts of its gargantuan body overdeveloped, while other bits were shrivelled mutant growths. *Geophagy during Pregnancy in Africa* would feel pretty lonely on its shelf, while the section devoted to magical and ritual sacrifice would be hugger-mugger squashed together. His was not the library of a gentleman of urbane and comprehensive interests. It suggested instead a reader who was most curious about things which ought not to have been of interest to him. Moreover, the shelves were so crowded that whole sections would have to be purged. He would find this painful, for it would be like dismembering a living thing.

The Creative Writing Working Party met a few days before term formally started. Lancelyn was a little late, and as he walked in, Wormsley greeted him,

'Ah! Here he is at last, Raven's pretty boy!'

Apart from Jaimie and Wormsley, there was a stranger in the room, a military-looking man with a moustache and an ugly haircut, but Lancelyn was not introduced to him, as Wormsley carried on with what he was saying about what would need to be covered in the writing course and the allocation of its teaching load. Lancelyn lit up a Black Russian.

'I wish you would not do that Lancelyn, either here or in the departmental meetings.'

'I only feel the need to smoke when I am bored.'

'"There are no uninteresting things, only uninterested people." Do you know who said that?... Chesterton. Has it ever occurred to you that, by making some small contribution to our discussions, you might alleviate the boredom to which you are so very sensitively a prey?'

Wormsley returned to outlining what the novel-writing part of the course would need to cover. Students would have to be taught how to shape the outline story and its subplots, how to open and close a story, how to brainstorm, how to manage conflicts, how to create tension, how to develop characters, how to edit, and, finally, how to market what they had written.

Having completed his summary outline of this part of the course, Wormsley then said, 'Of course, the beauty of it is that while they are learning how to be creative, or, doubtless in many cases failing to be creative, we are studying them and their attempts at creativity.'

At this point, the military-looking man coughed.

'Oh, I forgot to introduce you… this is Dr Robert Craik from Dundee. He is a cognitive psychologist. Our interests overlap, since he is interested in the psychology of creativity, whereas I am interested in the theology of creativity.'

Craik waved his hand at Lancelyn, who then said, 'What the hell is the theology of creativity? Are students on creative writing courses supposed to be lost souls and is learning how to write properly going to lead them to salvation?'

'Well, hell does come into it. But I am not really interested in producing writers. There are far too many out there already. Who cares if the student gets his crappy novel or poem published? I certainly don't. I am after bigger game. I am proposing a study of the mind of God the Novelist. Naturally such a potentially blasphemous investigation needs to be approached indirectly and so one starts by studying the inverse of God the Novelist, which is to say the novelist as god. Henry Fielding once boasted that he could have personally got his creation, Tom Jones, out of jail if he had wanted to, but that was not his way with his novel and so he refrained and Tom had to find his own salvation within the book. That is also God's way with the world, for we do not sense His presence here anymore than the characters in a novel are aware of the novelist's guiding and shaping hand in the universe that they find themselves in. God, in structuring our world, our history and our future, uses every literary trick in the book and more tricks than a human mind can dream of. God, like the novelist creates things *ex nihilo*. They both imagine a thing and it is. What they have conceived of in an instant is then experienced in the respectively imagined worlds as a sequence of events. So, you see, we are going to rescue God from the Theology Department.'

Wormsley looked triumphantly round the room. Jaimie looked as though he wanted to scratch his head. Dr Craik was impassive. Lancelyn thought about all this for a few minutes and then asked, 'What kind of God the Novelist is it who is all too ready to let small children suffer abominably?'

'That, if you will forgive me, is a stupid question. A Thomas Hardy kind of novelist is the answer. Remember the children hanged in *Jude the Obscure*: "Done because we are too menny"? Even the invocation of the sufferings of a hypothetical small child can give a novel an extra edge. Look at *The Brothers Karamazov*.'

'So God the Novelist keeps ramping up His plots in the hope of finding a publisher? I am sure He won't get Jonathan Cape. Maybe He should consider vanity publishing.'

Wormsley growled, 'You are a blasphemous sod! Do you know the real reason I did not want to see you appointed? It was because I knew that you were one of Burbottle's creatures.'

'What? Who the hell is Burbottle?'

'Yes. Well put. Hell is Burbottle – or Raven, as you presumably know him. You see, I knew Raven before the war, but he was not called Raven then. I knew him as the Reverend

Edward Burbottle.'

Lancelyn had a horrible sick feeling. Could this be true? Or was Wormsley going mad? He said, 'He was teaching mathematics before the war, but hoping to switch to astrophysics, and then he took part in the fighting in Italy.'

Wormsley laughed triumphantly.

'My poor, poor, credulous Lancelyn! And what a story! Burbottle spent most of the war years in prison. He knows no more mathematics than I do and he never was in Italy. He used to be a chaplain and religious education teacher at one of the minor Roman Catholic boarding schools, I forget which one, but he was also a shirt-lifter, and after being convicted of sexual assaults against young boys, he was jailed.'

'He told me that he had fought in Italy and that he discovered God while hiding in a monastery in the Apennines.' This had to be true.

'Oh really? What a load of old cock! But he is an inventive storyteller. I will give him that. Clever too. By the way he is an old Etonian, like you, and later he got to know M.R. James, when James was Provost of Eton.'

'None of this can be true,' said Lancelyn.

But he knew that it was. And Wormsley was relentless, 'Then don't take it from me. You can go and challenge him yourself. Having betrayed his vocation before the war, he went on to create a new identity as Raven and then to misapply a strictly religious discipline to literary criticism. So that what St Ignatius had intended as a way of leading a neophyte to God – and that in itself was a pernicious Papist exercise – was redesigned to take students on to publication and intellectual fame. That was the main reason why I did not want to appoint you, a product of Burbottle's perversion of what I judge to be a sinister form of religious devotion. By the way, did he ever feel you up?'

Jaimie looked interested, but Lancelyn waved that question away. It was not important, but, 'So why Raven?'

'I have no idea.'

Jaimie now looked as though he was about to say something. But at this point Craik called them to order. They seemed to have drifted some way from what should be the purpose of the meeting. Surely the aim of their great joint project was to track down the psychological origins of invention and fantasy. Craik did not envisage any need for laboratories or neurological probes. They just had to be patient observers who carefully watched how the students who tried to make fiction set about it. The brain's ability to invent things was one of the great mysteries of neuropsychology and Craik quoted from Sir Charles Scott Sherrington's *Man on His Nature*: 'The brain is waking and with it the mind is returning. It is as if the Milky Way entered upon some cosmic dance. Swiftly the head mass becomes an enchanted loom where millions of flashing shuttles weave a dissolving pattern, always a meaningful pattern though never an abiding one, a shifting harmony of sub-patterns.'

The mind weaves illusions or fictions, but in order for them to have any meaning those fictions have to be based upon reality and in the end the mind is the only instrument for the discovery of the truth. If it was possible through close observation to outline even a small part of the workings of the 'enchanted loom', then this would be exciting, but Craik concluded by saying that he did not think that any analogies with a Creation by a hypothetical Divinity were likely to be helpful.

Wormsley looked thunderous. As for Lancelyn, though he understood that there would be no need for laboratories, this still smelt like science and he was not sure that he liked it. Thereafter, with some difficulty, they returned to such bread-and-butter matters as the shape of the syllabus and how the observation of the students was going to be carried out.

An hour or so later, in the street Craik and Lancelyn looked at one another. Their eyebrows rose simultaneously.

'I don't think that I can get myself out of secondment to this one,' said Craik. 'But now I am thinking that it is not the students' minds that I should be investigating, but Wormsley's. That man is a megalomaniac. What is more, I think that if God existed (but He doesn't) He would be extremely angry to find himself being subjected to an extremely primitive form of psychoanalysis. Still, things are obviously much more colourful here than they are in Dundee. And I should love to meet the villainous Mr Raven. I envy you for having known him. As for Wormsley, before the meeting started, he was explaining to me how railway timetables were put together.'

With that, he raised his hand in farewell and departed.

He added Craik to the filing card system. By now thirty-five people had cards, all arranged in alphabetical order. But what was the point of that? He was not going to remember or find people in alphabetical order. He needed a more sensible taxonomy. First the division into sexes and then perhaps organisation by hair; abundance, or lack of it, and then hair colour. That would be a bit more sensible, even though he often found that he could not remember what a person's hair colour was. Then perhaps teeth.

When he returned home Lancelyn found that Molly had written him another letter.

> Darling Lancelyn,
>
> I have now read *The Prelude*. It was hard going, partly because the carbon copy was so faded and there were so many corrections on it. Maybe I have not read it carefully enough, but as far as I can see, there is no story here, because it has no end and it is not going towards any particular destination. Your telling me that **I** should provide the ending is a sodding cop-out. It is you who have to give it an ending and then it has to be properly published. I do not want to be the woman who inspired the carbon copy of a badly typed typescript. But in order for a publisher to take it, it has to have an ending and all that supernatural stuff will have to go. Never mind what bollocking Iron Foot Jack told you. Did you make him up? You must write about real life. Truth is always more interesting than fiction. And what is the point of changing Bernard's and my names? Publish the true story and let him sue if he dares. I think that you are rich enough to survive any libel costs, and if not, then let us go abroad and live in poverty. Tell our story as it really was. I do not mind becoming the woman at the centre of a scandal, since that would be so much better than remaining a mousey housewife. I will write to you about our next meeting.
>
> With my love and hope, Molly

It was hard to know how to respond to Molly's letter, not that he was allowed to write to her anyway. She was a difficult woman. Very hard to imagine her as a 'mousey housewife'. Voluptuously regal housewife possibly. Her eyes, breasts and thighs were part of his destiny. That had become obvious to him. But now, if he removed the magical element in the story as she wanted, then it was no story at all. Also, it was clear from Bernard's book that he did indeed admire Karswell, and therefore should Molly be believed when she poo-pooed the idea that Bernard might indeed have resorted to planting runes? But then, if runes had been planted, they were certainly slow-acting. Moreover, if Lancelyn described things as they had actually happened, then apart from it not being very interesting, he was increasingly aware that what narrative that remained brought little credit to himself. That book review should never have been written. Also, was Molly expecting him to include an account of their night together? Surely not? Now he thought about it though, he did not believe in magic, ghosts and supernatural stuff, and therefore it followed that, even if Bernard had been successful in hiding a piece of paper with some odd-looking scrawls on it in the library, so what? Then he wondered if a revised version of his youth would have to include an account of the successful impersonation as a war veteran and brilliant academic teacher by a convicted paedophile. But it now occurred to him that it was possible that it was Wormsley who was the inventive storyteller and that all the stuff about Burbottle, the homosexual chaplain, had been invented in order to wrong-foot him. Then it crossed his mind that perhaps he should consider including a summary of his fraudulent first version of *The Prelude* in the revised and truthful version of his life so far. Yes, oh dear, yes, the novel has an ending, but the ending of real people's lives was death, by which time they could not write about it. It was all too much to think about.

He found relief of a sort in resuming the teaching of the special subject. It was supposedly the job of the teacher to encourage students to challenge things and ask questions. Yet, in the first class of the new term he found himself introducing his class to Burton's warnings against curiosity. According to *The Anatomy of Melancholy*, curiosity was a kind of madness. Burton cited 'the tale of Pandora's box, which being opened through her curiosity, filled the world with all manner of diseases'. According to Burton: 'To these tortures of fear and sorrow may well be annexed curiosity, that irksome, that tyrannising care, *nimia solicitudo*, superfluous industry about unprofitable things and their qualities,' as Thomas defines it: 'an itching humour or a kind of longing to see that which is not to be seen, to do that which ought not to be done, to know that secret which should not be known, to eat of the forbidden fruit.'

Later, when Lancelyn was back in his library, it struck him as somewhat strange that the scholarly M.R. James, who was always investigating things and turning over libraries and archives, should in so many of his ghost stories warn against curiosity. There was 'A Warning to the Curious' of course. But then, in the story of 'Count Magnus', there was Mr Wraxall who stood in front of the mausoleum of the Count and was unwise enough to utter the words 'Ah, Count Magnus, there you are. I should dearly like to see you.' Then there was Parkins in 'Oh, Whistle, and I'll Come to You, My Lad', who found a something on the beach and when, late at night and back in the hotel, he thinks to examine it: 'It was with some curiosity that he turned it over by the light of his candles.' It was a whistle and after he blew upon it, a horrible visitation followed. And then there are Mr Somerton's cryptographic investigations in 'The Treasure of Abbot Thomas' which led to nothing good…

Maybe his mind had become so chaotic because his library was similarly so chaotic. He did after all think of his library as the exoskeleton of his brain.

His guide in the great reorganisation and re-shelving enterprise, was of course going to be Melvil Dewey's *Decimal Classification and Relativ Index*. He would start with all the books that should be grouped under 000, including taxonomy, library sciences, referencing and so forth and naturally that was where *Decimal Classification and Relativ Index* would in due course be shelved. Having made a start on this, he also started pulling books off the shelves that he judged should be in the 100s, philosophy and psychology. When he glanced at the books which might go in the 200s, religion, he thought it a little odd that so far he had not spotted a single copy of the Bible among his books. Doubtless one would turn up. Books were shape shifters which were always liable to change their size and colour of their covers from what one had so clearly remembered.

Old books are smelly things, but fortunately they smell much nicer than old men. There is something woody or smoky about the smell of old books. He could judge the age of a book just by smelling it. There was dust everywhere and dead bluebottles were now scattered all over the floor. Maybe in all this dusty chaos, he would happen upon that runic curse after all. Meanwhile the housekeeper would be angry. Come to think of it, he would bar her from entering the library for the foreseeable future.

He was too tired to make a start on the cleaning himself and as a break he started reading that biography of Dewey. He had intended to read only a chapter or two, and the early life of the world's greatest taxonomist seemed to be an inspiring story, but then, as he read on, doubts began to emerge and those doubts swelled until he found what he was confronted with so appalling that he still had to keep on reading until all the horrible, disillusioning truth was finally revealed. Dewey had been a racist, an anti-Semite, and though a misogynist, he was at the same time a man who hired women on the basis of their appearance and who then aggressively groped them. He also had a fanatical loathing of homosexuals. It was time to reconsider the Dewey Decimal system itself. Homosexuality was either 132, mental derangement or 159.9, abnormal psychology. As for women, they were a subsection of 395, etiquette. In the 200s, the religion section, Christianity took up almost all the numbers, leaving only the 290s, for non-Christian religions. Though Lancelyn sat there trying not to draw any conclusions from all this, he failed in this effort. The Decimal System was a tainted taxonomy. And now how should he re-shelve his books? But it was worse than that, for what also followed was that he needed to reorganise his brain and the way he saw the world. Things were starting to fall apart.

CHAPTER EIGHTEEN

He was in an ill humour when he joined the third meeting of the Creative Writing Working Party and for a while he was not really listening to what was being said. He was thinking about what he was about to propose. Finally, when the other three had noticed his silence, they in turn fell silent and waited for him to speak. He told them that he wished to add the option of autobiography and other forms of life writing to the creative writing course.

Wormsley demurred. Life writing was not truly creative, since it was merely a recording of things that had actually happened. Fiction was the thing. But Lancelyn told him that he was a fool to make such a hard-edged distinction between fiction and memoir. Correctly considered, non-fiction was just a specialised form of fiction. True, the biography or autobiography had to be seen to conform to reality and this was its constraint as an art form. But all sorts of poetry, such as the sonnet or the haiku, were also constrained by rules. Moreover, Wormsley should consider works of fiction that had passed themselves off as non-fiction, such as Defoe's *Robinson Crusoe* and *Journal of the Plague Year*. Also such notorious fakes as *Awful Disclosures of Maria Monk as Exhibited in a Narrative of Her Sufferings during a Residence of Five Years as a Novice* and Edward Backhouse's *China under the Empress Dowager*. Wormsley laughed and said that Burbottle would be a perfect supply teacher for this sort of thing as he was the expert in faking a life story, but then he said no to the proposal. The matter was closed and they should move on to other matters.

Lancelyn paid no attention and insisted on reading the advertisement for the life writing course that he had dashed off last night:

So you think you have had an interesting life? Prove it! Get your life out in print and amaze your friends and family.
You think you can't? Don't worry! We can give you the confidence that you <u>do</u> have it in you!

Our skilled mentors are excited to be offering you this opportunity to explore your hidden depths. (Yes, everybody has hidden depths.) First there are those intimate little secrets about such things as how you go to the lavatory, your phobia about sitting on a lavatory seat that someone else has just sat on, how you pick your nose and your masturbatory fantasies. But frankly those things are not so very important or interesting. We are offering you the chance to find out who you really are. It will be a roller-coaster-ride of self-discovery in which you will explore your dark areas and come to terms with your shameful deeds and secret fears: maybe hatred of your parents; fear of women; adultery; betrayal of a friend; academic fraud; suspicion of black men; terror of occult powers; an excessive fondness for small children; a murderous hatred of your fellow man. Who knows? Think of the comfort of having everything out in the open and published to the world. So why not take our master classes in self-revelation and explore it all with us?

Find out how things really are. Imagine coming across the carcase of a dead mole and then, supressing the first gulp of horror, you edge towards it and survey the white heaving nest of maggots in its belly. Ah ha! So this is what is in wait. This is how things are.

Apply: Creative Writing, Life Writing Skills c/o Professor Wormsley, English Department, University of St Andrews, St Andrews, Scotland.

Craik laughed. No one else did.

'You look tired, Lancelyn.'

'God, yes, I am so weary of it all.'

'Go home, Lancelyn. We will talk about this tomorrow.'

Back at the house he thought that he would find solace in continuing to sort out his books. Really there was no alternative to the Dewey Decimal System. Its warped value system must necessarily determine the organisation of his knowledge. Though he could put the book on geophagy under 'wining and dining', he supposed that he should put it in the woman bit of the Etiquette section. But so far there were no other books about women in that subsection, and now he thought about it, there seemed to be no books by women in his library. Odd that. Perhaps he should get his motorbike out and go over to Dundee and see if there was a bookshop there that would sell him a book by a woman? He did have Proust's *A la recherche du temps perdu*, but he was wondering if he should shelve the volumes under 132, or 159.9. Also, what about Jewish books? Should they have their own special section? There were many puzzles to keep him occupied.

He had little time to ponder these matters, for there was a loud knocking at the door. What now? It was Jaimie. This was only his second visit to the house, but this time he was not alone. Sylvie was with him, and though there was something strange about her appearance, Lancelyn was too preoccupied with other matters to register what it was at first and he wearily ushered them into the library. Jamie was astonished by all the literary chaos on the floor. Sylvie on the other hand, seemed to be surprised at how many books were still on the shelves. Jaimie fished in his briefcase.

'I have come to lend you a book,' he said.

'That is just what I need,' replied Lancelyn, pointing to the piles that made their progress to the chairs difficult.

'Aye, but you only need to read the first five or six pages. What is going on here? Are you moving?'

Lancelyn shook his head and navigated his way to the corner cupboard to get them some drinks. Once they were all sitting down, he began to read, and this is some of what he read in its opening pages:

The library, although duly considered in many alterations of the house and additions to it, had nevertheless, like an encroaching state, absorbed one room after another until it occupied the greater part of the ground floor. Its chief room was large, and the walls of it were covered with books almost to the ceiling; the rooms into which it overflowed were of various sizes and shapes, and communicated in modes as various – by doors, by open arches, by short passages, by steps up and steps down.'

Lancelyn read on. In this library books had a way of vanishing and reappearing and it was haunted by a Mr Raven, long time librarian to Sir Upward, the founder of the library:

'Sir Upward was a great reader... not only of such books as were wholesome for men to read, but of strange, forbidden or evil books; and in so doing, Mr Raven who was probably the Devil himself, encouraged him. Suddenly both disappeared, and Sir Upward was never after seen or heard of, but Mr Raven continued to show himself in the library.'

The novel was *Lillith* and it had been published in 1895 by George MacDonald. Lancelyn looked to Jaimie who told him to read just a little more. A little later Vane, the current owner of the library, found himself gazing into a mirror which, instead of showing him his reflection, revealed wild country beyond its glass and the first creature he saw there was 'hopping toward me with solemnity, a large and ancient raven, whose purply black was here and there softened with gray'.

Again Lancelyn looked to Jaimie, who meanwhile had picked up a copy of *A Hundred and Twenty Days of Sodom* and said, 'I've got a copy of this. It's good isn't it? But a bit repetitive I thought.'

Lancelyn shook his head and waved the copy of *Lillith* at him.

'What the hell is this?'

'Have you got to the bit where the bird is looking for worms?'

Lancelyn nodded.

'That bird, of course, is Mr Raven,' said Jaimie. 'And yet he is also simultaneously Adam Cadmos, the first man and his first wife was not Eve, but Lillith. Though Lillith is evil, her blinding beauty will lead Vane to redemption, and as a result, she will find redemption herself.'

'Now that you have given the plot away, I am not sure that I need to read the novel.'

'You should. It's a braw book, I think. You would do well to heed its message, for it is a great Scottish parable about ultimate things: life, suffering, death and salvation. To sleep in Raven's house is to die and Vane has to learn how to die, for that is the only way of becoming truly alive. Anyway I thought you should have a look at it, because that is obviously where your teacher found his name. This strange book has meant something to him. Perhaps it should mean something to you.'

'I do not want to be redeemed by a fiction. I do not think that I can be.'

'Well, perhaps it does not matter… I really came because the others in the Creative Writing Working Party were worried about you. How does he seem to you Sylvie?'

'I think he looks very nice.'

Jaimie raised his hand as if he were about to hit her, but then he slowly lowered it and said, 'I mean does he look in good health,' and to Lancelyn he said 'She was training to be a nurse.'

'But I failed the exams,' she contributed helpfully. 'Still I could take his pulse, I suppose.'

'If this is a health check, drink your drinks and then please go away. I am fine.'

'No. The truth is that was not the only reason for dropping by. Sylvie wanted to meet you properly and I wanted to give you something, something apart from that MacDonald novel.'

Again he fished in his briefcase.

'It's also a novel and it's mine. It is not finished and I don't think that I will ever bother to finish it, but I enjoyed the writing and I wondered what you would think of it. If I could leave it with you, there is no hurry in returning it.'

The novel, what there was of it, had been bound like a student's special subject thesis and neatly labelled *The World of Fiona MacAlpine*.

'It has turned out different from what I had expected,' said Jaimie. 'It now has so many characters in it that I have difficulty remembering who they are, and if I have that difficulty, it is going to be even worse for my readers.'

Would a card index be the answer? Another solution presented itself.

'You could have them all wearing badges with their names on,' suggested Lancelyn.

'That is a good idea – wait a moment. No, it is not.' And

Jamie looked suspiciously at Lancelyn.

'I am Fiona,' said Sylvie. She seemed resigned to this.

'You are the heroine,' said Jaimie.

'I wish the men did not keep doing things to me. Also she seems a bit stupid.' And then she pointed to the books on the floor. 'What is all this?'

'Just a bit of spring cleaning.'

'But it's only January.'

'I am impatient to get it over with.'

'I could help by coming over and doing a bit of dusting.'

It now struck Lancelyn that there was something elfin about her appearance. Both she and Jaimie could be envisaged as ambassadors from the faery folk.

There was a long silence. Finally Jaimie said, 'I think we should be going. The Prof wants you to take a few days off. Other members of the department can cover for you. I'll probably look in again tomorrow.'

He marched out of the house, but Sylvie lingered a moment at the door and this gave Lancelyn the chance to ask her, 'Why did you stick your tongue out at me a few months back?'

'So you'd notice me.'

'Believe me, I noticed you the first time I saw you.'

Whereupon she gave him the most glorious smile before hurrying after Jaimie. There were years of innocent girlhood in that smile and then something much less innocent. Lancelyn belatedly realised that the marks on her face were bruises. But he had no time to think about that. He gazed in on the disordered library with mingled pleasure and disgust, in the way that one might look upon an aged whore who had once given pleasure. After that he hurried to the phone in the hallway. He was now resolved to seek absolution from Bernard and he put a call through to All Souls. The person in the office told him that Bernard was no longer with the college, though she was unable to say why or when he had left, nor could she give him Bernard's home address. So then Lancelyn rang Raven to get the address of that cottage in Headington. But Raven, who wanted very much to talk about other things, would not give Lancelyn Bernard's address. He said that even if he could remember the address of the house, he still could not tell Lancelyn where Bernard was. Then Lancelyn said that he would come and look in on Raven once the St Andrews term was finished, but Raven replied that he feared that might be too late, and though he was unable to explain why, he was obdurate that Lancelyn must come as soon as possible, if he hoped to see him in Oxford, and really that would have to be before the end of the week. Lancelyn hesitated before replying that he would call sometime in the afternoon of the day after tomorrow. Raven hoped that this might not be too late.

CHAPTER NINETEEN

On the train down to London he started reading *The World of Fiona MacAlpine*.

Fiona and her husband, a wealthy Chinese mandarin, were in for a surprise (and so was Lancelyn). The Burns Night celebration was held in a ramshackle building, which though it was called The White Heather Hotel, seemed oddly organised for such an establishment. Rory, its owner, greeted Fiona enthusiastically, while merely nodding at the mandarin. Then they and thirty or more diners of various races were piped in and told to sit where they liked, except not together. Some of those who took their places at the long table wore masks. Not only was there plenty of whisky, but opium pipes were being passed up and down the table. Once the Scotch broth had been served, it became confusing as to who was or was not a guest, since every now and then a diner would vacate his seat which would promptly be occupied by a manservant or a maid, and then the former diner would take on the role of a servant. Still everything seemed almost normal. The haggis was piped in and an Englishman – whom Fiona's husband recognised from having done business with him – rose to make 'The Address to the Haggis' and having finished this fine poem, he made to cut the haggis lengthwise. Whereupon it exploded and bits of haggis ended up on many of the assembled diners.

It was now decreed that the Englishman must be punished. This happened with surprising speed. He was manacled and made to kneel in front of the table and splinters of bamboo were forced under his fingernails before being set alight. Though he made no sound, rivers of sweat ran down his face. This was much admired.

Since the fragments of exploded haggis had ruined many pretty dresses, this was a signal for the women to start to strip. Fiona was told that it was her turn to serve at the table and that she too should take her dress off. When she hesitated, the dress was ripped off her and she was beaten with a bamboo stick, but so gently that it left no marks on her skin. As for her mandarin husband, when he protested he was seized and held until a large metal contraption had been wheeled in. A metal bucket seat was suspended from its frame and he was strapped onto this. His head was then shaved as a prelude to the activation of a mechanism at the top of the frame which proceeded to scatter drops of water at random intervals on the mandarin's head. At first the foolish mandarin welcomed the coolness of the water, but this was of course the notorious Chinese water torture. Once this was under way, servants (or were they guests?) wheeled a bed into the middle of the dining chamber so that the mandarin would be able to see all that was to take place. 'You are now my number one woman and we make lovey-dovey,' Rory told Fiona. She submitted gratefully since she had enjoyed being whipped, as all women do, so long as their flogging is administered with due moderation.

Used as he was to seventeenth-century prose, Lancelyn found Jaimie's style rather staccato. Also, apart from Fiona and Rory, all the celebrants at the feast were anonymous. He started to skim the rest. Jaimie's narrative continued with accounts of the bastinado, the steel-bladed chair, eye gouging and the death of a thousand cuts, among other things. The following morning the partially demented mandarin had been released from his throne of torment, but though he expected Fiona to follow him out of the hotel, she clung affectionately to Rory and waved her husband bye-bye. Whereupon he made his way to the old Shanghai fortress and jumped from its highest tower. When news of his suicide reached The White Heather Hotel, Rory told Fiona that the mandarin had jumped to his death in order to make them feel guilty. Yet there could be no question of that, he said, and instead they would hold another and bigger party.

In London Lancelyn took a room at the Hilton. It was difficult to sleep and he turned with some relief from *The World of Fiona MacAlpine* to *Lillith*. When he did fall asleep he had another of his relentlessly boring dreams. He had been waiting at a bus stop and there was an old man beside him, who pointed urgently at a street urchin across the road, and without any conversational preamble said, 'That boy has no heart.' Lancelyn could not face any delay. The bus was already running late, and now it had arrived, he boarded it. He awoke worrying about his class and what they would make of his absence. After breakfast, he had to fight off the urge to postpone the trip to Oxford and the encounter with Raven by touring the bookshops of Charing Cross Road. It had started to rain by the time he arrived in Oxford. He had to knock loudly several times on Raven's door before Raven opened it. He seemed surprised to see him. Behind him was a scene of chaos with books piled all over the floor. Had he also decided to reorganise and re-shelve his books? Then Lancelyn spotted the tea chests through the door in the bedroom. There was a smell about the place.

'Ah yes, well… welcome,' said Raven. 'Have you come to help? I can't find anything. I would offer you a drink if I could remember where the bottle has got to. As it is, we will have to do with sober conversation. What would you like to talk about?'

And he cleared a couple of seats of miscellaneous bric-a-brac and stationery. Looking at Raven, Lancelyn thought that extreme old age had suddenly come upon the man like a curse. As he moved about, he was hunched forward, so that his eyes were fixed upon his shuffling feet and his mutterings could have been mistaken for the soft gibbering of a monkey. 616.83.

Lancelyn finally spoke, 'As I said on the phone, I need to get in touch with Bernard. I badly want to talk to him. I owe him an apology.'

Raven sat silent, pondering something. Then he said, 'Ah yes, now I've got it. I guess that it must be that humorous review you wrote in the *TLS*.'

'How did you know that it was my work?'

'The Bedouin of the Arabian desert can read the tracks of

a camel in the sand. From looking at a single hoof print, they deduce the age and sex of the beast, whether it was heavily loaded, when it last ate, which tribe it belonged to, and how fast it was traveling. As they say, "The track cannot lie." It is the same with English prose. Your prose rhythms, with their variation of parataxis and hypotaxis, are like the camel's hoof prints. They advertise your identity. It has long been my art to identify the perpetrators of a whole range of sentence structures.'

'Gosh! Did you never think of writing yourself? Your wartime experiences would make a wonderful story, with that contrast between all the bangs, blood and guts of the fighting and the deep peace of the monastery in the Apennines.'

'Oh dear yes, but that was all so long ago and there are already so many books. But now we must wait for someone… late, whoever it is. Now you must excuse me if I close my eyes for a few moments.'

The few moments turned into a bit over half an hour. Then someone did arrive. It was Molly and she hugged Lancelyn, while Raven slowly came to and then bustled about. At length he located a bottle of port, as well as an ashtray for Lancelyn. Another chair was cleared for Molly.

'There we are,' said Raven. 'Now what were we talking about?'

Dementia had been placed by Dewey in 616.83 along with other diseases of the central nervous system.

'I have come to Oxford to find Bernard,' said Lancelyn, looking at Molly. She shrugged and indicated that he should look to Raven for an answer. Raven contemplated Lancelyn as if he were trying to decide what kind of answer would satisfy him. The decision was made.

'You probably know that Bernard was not getting on with the senior dons at All Souls. All that Barthes nonsense and whatnot. And then that review. When he got wind of the fact that his research fellowship was not going to be renewed, he lit out.'

'So where did he lit out to?'

'I like to think that, wanting the encouragement of preferment, and besides, finding himself friendless, he now makes his way through woods, over moors and across streams, and having shunned the sort of learning that can be found in books, and guided by the winds and the chatter of birds, he studies to read the language of water, wood and stone. With the dust of academia washed off by the season's rains, he has made himself a scholar gypsy, a master of the arts of nature. At least, that is what I am hoping.'

'Oh, fuck it! Wouldn't you just know that now he has left me, he has stopped being so boring,' said Molly bitterly. 'We don't know where he is. The bastard has gone and left no message.'

'But that was not what we were talking about while we were waiting for… er… you…' Raven smiled at Molly who had been taking notes on what he had been saying. 'Ah, yes, the monastery in the Apennines. Now that the College has released me from my duties, I think I should rather like to visit it once more. Father Jacopo was very old, yet I hope there may still be some who remember me there.'

'Do you never think of revisiting your old friend, the Reverend Edward Burbottle?'

'Who on earth is Burbottle? He is nothing to me.'

'You are lying. Your name is not really Raven. You told me when we last met that Raven was the name that you adopted after the War.'

'On the contrary, I am now telling you the truth when I say that Burbottle is nothing to me. It is true that we have successively occupied the same body. It is my misfortune to have been allotted the second part of this body's life span, whereas he had all the joys of youth – and many youths did he enjoy! As for myself, I have made my own future. So why then should I not remake my past so that it might better accommodate my future? After all, "Burbottle" was no kind of name for a Man of Power.'

Lancelyn did not immediately reply to all this, since he thought he should first spell out to Molly Raven's inglorious past as a school chaplain, child molester and convict.

Once Lancelyn had finished, Raven nodded approvingly before continuing, 'The change of identity did not take place when the name of this body was officially changed. It was before that. It took place in prison where the miserable wretch Burbottle soon found himself appointed to the post of prison librarian. While there, that evil but ingenious man read a lot of novels and having read MacDonald's extraordinary story, *Lillith*, he realised that change was possible. He decided in a sense to die, as Vane dies, and then to make himself a new character in a life that should resemble a novel. Not only that, but all the important people in his future life should be as if they were characters in a novel – his novel, which became my novel. So it was that, at some point during this stint as prison librarian, he became I. I fancy this transformation mirrored in reverse that famous story of Robert Louis Stevenson, so that now the villainous Mr Hyde was transformed into the virtuous Dr Jekyll. Having accomplished so much, I believed that I could make life more generally follow fiction, not realising it was a hopeless task, since few people's lives will obey the rules of the novel… you and Bernard were my best hope… too slow.'

'When we last met, you spoke of a pattern.'

'Was I really so indiscreet? When was that? Yes, the pattern, the pattern… I have it now, or rather I have had it…'

Perhaps he did momentarily see the pattern in his mind, but at this point Molly interrupted,

'I trusted you and I thought I could tell you everything – and I did. But you kept almost everything from me!'

'Most remiss of me. We all have our secrets, including you. But did I forget to tell you that… him over there wrote that review of *Towards a Reinvention of Edwardian…* something or other?'

Molly's hand went to her mouth. Finally she said, 'I never even read that bloody review.' Then, turning to Lancelyn she said, 'Bernard kept reading that review. When he first read it, he wept. But he forced himself to read it again and again and eventually he decided that it was right and then it made him laugh.'

'So nearly there,' said Raven. 'It has almost made sense.'

It could now be seen that a small pool of urine was gathering at Raven's feet. He looked down on it, yet though he was plainly dismayed at what he saw, he continued, 'Something Robert Louis Stevenson wrote points the way to us: "The web then, or the pattern; a web at once sensuous and logical, an elegant and pregnant texture: that is style, that is the foundation of the art of literature." Our lives are no work of literature, but they can and should become one. I... we just needed more time... and more energy. There may still be echoes, but from now on they will not mean anything. The pattern that is the reflection... God the artist... but then the disenchantment of the world. But tell me, from whom did you learn about Burbottle?'

'Professor Wormsley.'

'Wormsley... Wormsley... Wormsley, yes. I met him when he was a junior lecturer in Oxford. Soon after the war we met at a meeting of the Inklings at the Bird and Baby. Neither of us was an Inkling, but we sat outside the ring of those grand figures, Lewis, Tolkien, Barfield, Dyson, Coghill, a few others whose names I forget... after they had gone home, we still sat drinking and I got very drunk, and finding him simpatico and like-minded, I told him everything. I spoke about the past self that I had slewed off like a chrysalis, as well as my ideas about turning the study of literature into a spiritual discipline and ultimately bringing the student to the face of God. Do you know what Hugo Dyson had said to me?... neither do I. I have forgotten. But I do remember that beer-soaked religious discourse that Wormsley and I shared. I thought that I had discovered a kindred soul. A few days later I encountered him in the High and he was extraordinarily rude to me. That was the end of that.'

Molly put her notebook aside and looked to Lancelyn and said, 'With Bernard gone, I have not been able to keep up with the rent on the house and now I am sleeping on a friend's floor. I want to come with you. I have had enough –'

Raven interrupted, 'You two are young. You should pity

me, for I was never a boy or a young man and the wretched Burbottle, who had the looks, has bequeathed to me a creaking and sickening body. *Damnosa hereditas*. Look at me! Look at me!'

Nevertheless Molly continued, 'I have had enough revelations for one afternoon. Can I come and live with you and can we go *now* please?'

Lancelyn nodded. They rose simultaneously and headed for the door. Raven started to shuffle after them. So then they hurried down the stairs and raced through the rain across Mob Quad. It was exhilarating to be running away from old age and death! Life! Life and Youth! All was before them. Once out of the college they slowed down and conferred. Molly went off to collect some of her things from the friend she had been staying with and then more stuff that had been in store with another friend. They arranged to meet at Kings Cross the following morning. Lancelyn spent another night at the Hilton.

The following day at the Kings Cross ticket office, Molly wanted to know if they really had to go to St Andrews, but Lancelyn replied, 'My books. I must make arrangements for my books. Then we can go wherever you like... Acapulco... Paris... Delhi.'

Seated opposite to her on the train to Edinburgh, Lancelyn wondered if it was indeed Molly who was going to fulfil Raven's prophecy and break his heart. He presumed so, and the way Raven had talked, it was something that he should be looking forward to. Molly, for her part, had suddenly become anxious that Bernard might be on their train, having been shadowing them ever since the previous day. Lancelyn dismissed the idea, but added, 'I don't believe all that wandering gypsy stuff. He is probably staying with one of his aunts in Hartlepool.'

She smiled and shrugged.

'Oh well, I am glad he has gone. Failure doesn't interest me. Failure is always boring.'

'So you have given up on being a muse?'

'What on earth are you talking about? Why would anyone want to become a muse? Oh yes, maybe I did say something like that… but that sounds to me like an intellectualised version of a housewife. Right from the beginning, when we first encountered each other in that pub I could see that you and Bernard were perfect material. I needed to look no further. I have never stopped wanting to be a novelist and I have continued to take notes to that end. Over our lunches Raven used to advise me on how to set about it, though he failed to guess that he was also going to be in my book. He was too preoccupied with grooming me to become your mistress. Still, I like the sound of "mistress". Much better than "muse" or "housewife".'

It was a long journey to Edinburgh, and thinking it might amuse her, he produced *The World of Fiona MacAlpine* and encouraged her to read some of it. She was amused and after a while they started reading it aloud to each other and laughing and getting dirty looks from fellow passengers. They were both in a most odd state of mind that allowed them to find so much mirth in Rory's supervision of a death by a thousand cuts. Molly's final verdict on Jaimie's unfinished book was that it was 'charming and strangely innocent'.

Once out of Edinburgh and on the little branch line to St Andrews, Molly fell asleep. So she missed the beautiful deserted beaches of Burntisland and Kinghorn and the angry sea that still glittered in the gathering dark. Lancelyn let his spirit brood over the waters before turning to gaze on Molly. Her beauty promised an escape from the ordinariness of manhood. In the words of de la Mare, 'Woman, the mysterious, but yet not-quite-impossible She... she is memory and strangeness, earth's delight, death's promise. In a thousand shapes and disguises she visits us.' All that and welcoming smiles, soft flesh and the smell of intimacy. In a sense he had failed in his mission to Oxford. He had not found Bernard and therefore he had not found absolution. Yet now he exulted in his failure, for she was really all he had wanted and now he had her. He was like a big game hunter who was bringing back his trophy. What on earth had he done in his short life to deserve her?

Once they had arrived in Hepburn Gardens, they dumped all Molly's stuff in the hall.

'And now we shall go to bed.'

Lancelyn feared that she might be wanting to research a sex scene for her mysterious novel, but he swiftly decided that he would be happy to help her in that. The following day they both awoke early and took a morning walk while the light was still pearly grey. Hand in hand they passed the ruins of the castle and the cathedral on their way to the East Sands. They kissed at the end of the pier. Dawn was late and slow in arriving. Even under the heavy clouds there was light and the place was so beautiful. Surely here they could be happy for the rest of their time together? He would introduce her to the decorous peace of this medieval town, and then reading together, walking on the beaches and the Lade Braes, making love, having children and later family picnics in the Forest of Tentsmuir, and finally, ageing gently, they would come to embrace the daily sweetness of life. Bernard was only a distant danger. Lancelyn liked to imagine him, as like Satan, walking backwards and forwards across the country.

CHAPTER TWENTY

When they got back to the house, Jaimie was sitting, waiting on the doorstep. He smiled at them and said, 'Good morning to you both. It is a dreich day. May I come in?'

'Good morning, Jaimie. This is Molly. Come in, won't you?'

They followed Lancelyn into the kitchen where he set about making coffee.

'I'm Professor Wormsley's spy,' Jaimie explained to Molly. 'Lights were seen in the house last night, so we knew that Lancelyn must be back.' Then to Lancelyn, 'We have been worried about you. Where have you been?'

Lancelyn ignored the question and instead said, 'We have both been reading your novel. It is terribly exciting.'

Molly nodded enthusiastically and Jaimie looked pleased.

'Och! Well I dinna intend for anyone but you to read it,

Lancelyn. It was just an experiment. I have been teaching literature in this place for three years now and it only recently struck me that I did not actually know how fiction got made. That was like lecturing on Renaissance art without knowing anything about paints, paintbrushes or canvases. Anyway, now I know and I can see that it is easy. But I have made some revisions. Perhaps you would like to read the improved version?' He smiled at Molly. 'You are welcome to read it too.' Then to Lancelyn, 'It was something Wormsley said during that first meeting of the Creative Writing Working Party that really got me going. "The novelist must be cruel to his characters." He had me read *Jude the Obscure* and *Tess of the D'Urbervilles*. They were interesting, but a bit tame. Then I thought that maybe I could do better than that.'

Molly wanted to know how his fucking brilliant story would finish. Jaimie said that he could not be bothered to finish it. He had learnt what he needed from his experiment at being creative. Anyway why should the story he had been writing ever have an ending? Lancelyn wanted to know about his classes? It was a bit late to worry about that now. Henry would be taking over at least the next couple of week's teaching. (Oh dear.)

Jaimie said he would call back the following morning with the revised version. He had had some further afterthoughts. Then Molly said that though she had been writing a novel too, she was not ready to show it to anyone. After Jaimie was gone, she remarked on how pretty he was and added that she thought that what Jaimie really needed was not critical reading but mothering. It belatedly struck Lancelyn that Jaimie's good looks were really not so much boyish as Beardsleyesque.

It was like being under an idyllic version of house arrest. They were still in bed when towards the middle of the morning Jaimie was heard banging on the door. He read parts of his revised version to Lancelyn and Molly while they had their breakfast. Though a lingering account of a disembowelment hardly seemed to go with this meal, they managed the feat. A lot more adjectives had been stuck into the revised version. Also Jaimie had got Rory to insist that everyone who entered the whorehouse must wear a badge with his or her name on it, because Rory was no good at remembering faces and names. It was getting quite complicated, who was torturing or raping whom. So the badges were, after all, a good idea. Also Fiona MacAlpine now had luxuriant black hair.

Jaimie said, 'I didn't think I had any imagination.'

Since it was Saturday Jaimie had no teaching and he asked Lancelyn if he could explore the library. Of course. A little later he and Molly fell upon Pauline Réage's *The Story of O*, the story of a female fashion photographer who is step by step reduced to the status of a branded sexual slave. (So there was a book by a woman in the library!) They decamped with this novel to the sofa next door, where they took turns in reading bits out to each other and just occasionally they acted little bits out. Meanwhile Lancelyn paced restlessly about the house. As for Jaimie and Molly, after a while they read no more.

Darkness was falling and it was clear that a storm was coming by the time Jaimie made his farewells. Once he was gone, Lancelyn told Molly that he did not believe that Wormsley had sent him round that day. Rather, it was Molly he had come to see. But Molly told him that it was Lancelyn that Jaimie really fancied. Indeed, she was quite jealous. Still

Lancelyn wished that he would stop coming round. Then, 'Divorce Bernard and marry me.'

She shook her head so emphatically that her hair veiled her face.

'But we can be happy together. You know that.'

'I don't want a happy life. I want an interesting one. Bernard was a mistake. I don't want you to be my next one. Besides if we did get married, I would find that I was wedded to a library.'

The following morning, the Sunday, it was still raining heavily and so Jaimie did not arrive till noon, by which time there was only drizzle. He came with a suitcase and apologetically smiled at them. The roof of his cottage had partially collapsed and he had had to call in builders to get the roof mended. Would it be all right if he spent a few nights in Hepburn Gardens? That would be fine and Lancelyn suggested that Sylvie should join them too, but Jaimie said that someone needed to look after the cottage and let the builders in. She would be quite comfortable sleeping on a mattress in the kitchen, whereas he had a busy week's teaching ahead and would need his sleep. He was shown the spare room where he should leave his suitcase.

Jaimie and Molly read a little more of *The World of Fiona MacAlpine*, before starting to search the library for something different. Lancelyn overheard Molly saying to Jaimie, 'Don't you think his books feel wrong? This is the library of an old man. It should go with white hairs and a stooping posture.'

Eventually the two of them settled upon *Story of the Eye* by Georges Bataille, a novel of adolescent passions, orgies and disembodied eyes. Lancelyn tried and failed to persuade them to join him in a walk in the drizzle. So he went out alone.

Soon after dinner Jaimie went to bed early, saying that the following day would be busy. Molly and Lancelyn sat up for a while and argued about whether they should get a television or not. The matter was still unresolved when they retired. When Lancelyn woke in the middle of the night he found that he was alone in the bed. He stayed awake a long time as he hoped for her return. Jaimie went out very early, having left a note saying that he would be back late in the afternoon.

It was time to confront Molly.

'What is going on?'

'Do I really have to spell it out?'

'But I love you and I thought that you loved me.'

'I do love you... sort of. You are lovely and I am very fond of you, but he has a kind of power that I am unable to resist. I don't love him the way I love you, but he exerts this pull. It is like a tide which I cannot swim against. You should feel sorry for me.'

Lancelyn went for another walk.

Late in the afternoon Jaimie reappeared and he was carting another suitcase. A quarter of an hour later Sylvie arrived with a wheelbarrow loaded with stuff. Jaimie helped her unload it and carry the contents into the hallway. The main item was a record player with some records. Then Sylvie walked on into the library, saying, 'I wish I lived in a big house.' Then, as if the thought had struck her afresh, 'What a lot of books!'

Jaimie moved to usher her out of the house. Her last words were, 'But it's hardly leaking at all.'

Then Jaimie and Molly began to shift the piles of books on the library floor out into the hall and they got Lancelyn to help them. Jaimie set up the record player and put a record of Scottish dance music on the turntable. He was going to teach Molly some Ceilidh dances, starting with 'The Dashing White Sergeant' and 'The Pride of Erin Waltz'. Jaimie invited Lancelyn to join them but he went and sat in a corner and watched. Eventually he wearied of this and announced that he was going to bed. They looked irritated to have their fun so abruptly interrupted.

Molly said, 'Oh, I forgot to tell you… the bed Jaimie and I slept on last night is not really large enough. So while you were out I moved your stuff out into that bedroom and then his stuff into yours which has got a nice double bed.'

'You can't do that!'

'I just have.'

'OK, that's it. I am ordering you both to leave this house right now. I don't care where you sleep, as long as it is not in this house.'

'Don't be silly Lancelyn. You have told me that you love me. Indeed I have heard you mutter that you would die for me, and yet when we ask you for this one small thing, it seems that you do not love me that much after all. Don't you want me to be happy? You are looking all sulky. So sweetly sulky. Are you not pleased to see me so happy? Let me kiss you goodnight.'

And she closed in on him and gave him a big kiss on the mouth. It was true. He could deny her nothing. Jaimie was smiling. It now struck Lancelyn that there was something ever so faintly goat-like in Jaimie's handsome appearance, but then perhaps he was reading the man's prose into his face.

The Highland music kept Lancelyn awake for a couple of hours.

When Jaimie next appeared early in the evening of the following day, Lancelyn asked him how things were in the department.

'We are all missing you and hoping that you soon get over whatever it is that you need to get over. Wormsley makes a show of exulting in your signs of nervous strain, yet I think that he is really sorry to be out of touch with his favourite adversary and he is taking it out on the rest of us. I hear that Henry is making a pig's ear of teaching your class. But perhaps you can help me out with mine. Tomorrow I have to lecture on *Private Memoirs and Confessions of a Justified Sinner* by James Hogg. He was the Ettrick Shepherd, if you remember. I've done him before of course, but rather than blether on in the same way as last year, I think it's time I said something new about the book and about the problem of evil that is at the centre of its concerns. It's an early nineteenth-century masterpiece of Scottish fiction. Robert Wringhim believes he can commit any crime and yet he is predestined to salvation because he is the member of a chosen elite and so, at the urging of his devilish doppelgänger Gil-Martin, he commits many crimes, but yet he believes that he will be forever without sin. Perhaps there is such an elite. I don't know. I have often wondered. I wish Hogg had made his meanings plainer. It's the devil to teach. It's a wild book and it ends when Wringhim, under the deluded belief that he and Gil-Martin have a suicide pact, hangs himself. As Hogg tells it, the story is self-contradictory and makes no sense.'

Molly, who had just had a shower and who was wet and naked, came up behind Jaimie to hug him, but he shook her off and continued, 'Was he mad and if so was he therefore truly without sin? And, if mad, was it God or the Devil who had crazed him? Wild! I really wonder if we should allow madmen to be without blame, no matter what sins and follies they commit. But then I think that the commission of evil acts must be inextricably bound up with the freedom to commit those acts and there must always be something admirable about freedom. Are you with me on this? Also it has always struck me as strange that though I have read about plenty of evil people in novels – the Master of Ballantrae and Mr Hyde, for examples – I have never met one in real life. Have you?'

Lancelyn shook his head. Jaimie waited for more of a response from him, and then since Lancelyn seemed to be incapable of providing any insights into the theological and literary issues raised by the Hogg book, he strode off, muttering, 'And I had thought that you were really clever.'

Molly reappeared, and though damp and very cold, she insisted on sitting on Lancelyn's lap. She whispered in his ear, 'My darling, you think I do not love you anymore, but I do. I really do, and what is more, I know that Jamie would not be prepared to do half as much for me as you have already done. All will be well. Isn't life wonderful? It has always been you.'

Lancelyn admired her swaying buttocks as she strode away. He must do everything he could to assist her in breaking his heart. There was a kind of complicity in this.

After dinner Jaimie and Molly decided to play at re-enacting scenes from *The World of Fiona MacAlpine* – with Lancelyn's assistance of course. One of the things that had come over in the wheelbarrow was a red satin robe with a hood. There were also some whips and handcuffs. Molly donned the robe, and having done so, she demanded that Lancelyn should strip. He tried to refuse. But now she seemed really angry.

'Do you really love me, or don't you? Don't be so wet. This is just a game. You won't get seriously hurt. Darling, we love you, far too much for that.'

So it was that he ended up crawling on hands and knees round the floor of the library. Molly sat side-saddle on his back and from time to time she struck him lightly on the rump.

'I can't tell you how happy it makes me, to see how much you truly love me.'

When later they tried to persuade him to join them in the dancing lessons, he pleaded that he was far too exhausted. He retired to bed, but lay awake a long time. He had thought that Molly had previously cured him of his fear of women. It was now clear that she had greatly increased that fear. Was it possible to love and to fear someone at one and the same time? These sex games were all part of modernity. He was sure that Browne and Burton had known nothing of such romps.

CHAPTER TWENTY-ONE

Jaimie had no teaching the following morning. This was unfortunate. Their games resumed soon after breakfast. Then there was a knocking at the door. It was Henry who had come to seek advice on teaching the special subject. Lancelyn (who was fully dressed) tried to keep him in the hallway, but then Molly, with the scarlet robe flowing behind her and revealing most of her, rushed out, pursued by Jaimie who was wearing a black leather corset. Henry bolted. A little later the housekeeper arrived, but only to hand in her notice. She was tight-lipped about it. Then Molly wanted him to clear out the books from the bedroom. They were off-putting, as she imagined that they were like voyeurs. By now there was no space in the hall for more books, but they could go in a shed at the end of the garden. Lancelyn groaned.

'This is the school of love. You want us to look after you,

don't you? You need us.'

He had emptied a few shelves in the bedroom before deciding he needed some air. Now the beauty of the beaches and the town furnished the perfect backdrop for his misery. He was making his way along Market Street when a man propped up under the window of the toyshop stuck his leg out so that Lancelyn almost tripped over it. The man was sprawled on a thick overcoat and his straw boater was pulled forward to cover most of his face. A loosely knotted tie hung over a checked shirt. String was tied round bottom ends of the trouser legs. Was this a vagrant's version of spats? That part of the man's face that was still visible was unshaven and the mouth was smiling. There was an open can of McEwan's beer beside him. Surely it was Bernard? But no, when the man pulled his hat up it was obvious that he was not Bernard. This man was a tramp and a total stranger. He said, 'What are you looking at?'

Lancelyn shrugged.

'Well, look on. You see me happy as a sandboy, whereas you look bloody miserable.' He paused for thought. Then, 'Tell you what, I could do you a favour. We could change clothes and swap places. I will even throw in what's left of this beer as an extra. I bet I can do what you do and meanwhile you can settle down here with a drink in the sun and take over my happiness. Go on. You will never get an offer like this again.'

Lancelyn shrugged and walked on.

'You had your chance!'

Surely there was something swinish in the tramp's contented idleness, whereas though Lancelyn was suffering greatly, it was unmistakeably noble suffering that he experienced. He never got as far as the sea. He paused in the ruins of the Cathedral and looked up at St. Rule's Tower. Was it necessary for him to die, like Vane and Lillith, in order to truly become alive? Was this where Jaimie intended that he should finish his life? If so, he was going to be disappointed. Lancelyn had already told him that he did not believe in salvation through fiction. Perhaps Molly would have been sorry, probably not. Lancelyn had the feeling that, if Raven's pattern had worked, it would indeed have been Bernard sprawled on the pavement. But clearly there was now no pattern. Only false leads, useless coincidences, parallelisms that were not really so. Coincidences were of two types, meaningful and meaningless, and then there were encounters which mysteriously failed to fully manifest themselves as coincidences. The encounter with the tramp was a failed coincidence. Abruptly he changed his mind. He would after all change clothes with that man and give him the key to Hepburn Gardens. It was pleasant to think of Molly and Jaimie having to deal with this man.

But by the time he got back to Market Street the tramp had gone. On the spur of the moment Lancelyn decided to enter the toyshop. The proprietor was wearing the brown overall that so many shopkeepers in St Andrews wore.

'How may I help you sir?'

'I don't know. I am just so lonely.'

The proprietor stroked his chin and then reached into a drawer.

'I may have just the thing for you sir.'

He produced a piece of yellow fabric that had been sewn into the shape of a glove, except that it had only room for two fingers. Also there was a yellow head with little black ears and eyes. It was a bit like a bear, but not very.

'A glove puppet. It may keep you company.'

Lancelyn paid for it and walked on towards Hepburn Gardens. Lonely. The small number of his file cards and the perfunctory quality of the entries on them furnished conclusive evidence that he had no real friends. By now, he was experiencing his loneliness as something that had taken possession of his body. Perhaps Jaimie and Molly had noticed that he was lonely, for when he got back, they produced an inflatable sex doll which they said could keep him company in bed, but then seeing the glove puppet, Jaimie decided that the doll was probably not needed. They were gleeful, since they had found Lancelyn's hidden cache of porno magazines in the bedroom. Jaimie also had a message, 'Professor Wormsley wants to see you in his office at eleven tomorrow.'

'That may be too late.'

'Too late for what?'

'Too late for whatever is about to happen.'

'We will decide what is going to happen.'

What happened next was that later that night Molly decided that he should watch how a real man made love.

'I wonder if you really love me. Or do you just love your shitty love for me?'

An interesting question, but he was made to follow them into what was now their bedroom and told to sit under the window where he could get a proper view. He sat there listening with his eyes shut and when, a little later, he heard Jaimie's, 'I am, as they say, all mouth and no trousers,' he tried to stop his ears too. At length he was allowed to creep away unchallenged. He hoped that she was just testing him.

He could not remember what was supposed to happen on the following day. Remembering the future was problematic.

CHAPTER TWENTY-TWO

Though he was terribly tired, he did not go straight to bed, but went downstairs and sat in the library. There was a voice,

'Since you are young, you think that you will never die. But young people die like the old. It just takes them longer to get there.'

So there was someone in the library. It was a middle-aged man with clear almost boyish features. He was a trifle overweight and he wore large round steel-rimmed spectacles. He had the look of a clergyman, but a clergyman who was accustomed to exercise authority. Lancelyn knew that he must be looking at M.R. James and therefore he must have commenced an immersion in *Ghost Stories of an Antiquary*. Like Burton before him, James had been examining his library and had found some curious books in it. Lancelyn should not be so curious and neither should his books.

Lancelyn wondered why James had come to see him. James announced that whereas fictional ghosts should always be malevolent, real ghosts were merely postmen from the other world and the message that they carried was always the same. Death. They were perhaps like the hamsters that were given to small children to care for. Infallibly the death of the hamster would instruct the child about the reality of death.

It struck Lancelyn that James' reference to hamsters was incongruous. After all there were none in his ghost stories. Odder yet, there was now someone else in the room, who put his arm round James' shoulders and said, 'I'm Monty's china plate.'

'He means that I am his friend,' explained James. 'China plate is rhyming slang for mate.'

'I told you I would come if you needed me and blimey, you do need me, swelp me God,' said Iron Foot Jack. Your problem is the theft and bribery.'

'He means that your problem is your library.'

This was all far too ridiculous. Lancelyn started to laugh and he woke up laughing. He soon stopped laughing. This had been no immersion, but a dream, though a bit less boring than the usual ones. So a ghost within a dream of what he had believed to be a controlled vision. What did it mean to dream of a ghost? Could this indeed be a harbinger of death? Freud of course would be completely useless on the subject, but Lancelyn went over to the dreams and mysteries section, 135, of his still disordered library and found that according to Lefroufrou's Victorian *Egyptian Dream Book*, to dream of a ghost betokened unfinished business. Maybe so. But as he continued to think about it, he feared that in reality ghosts were comforting illusions, since their chief function was to veil the full horror of the vast and indifferent universe with its endlessly rotating dead planets, burnt-out stars and howling cosmic winds.

He went into the kitchen for a bowl of porridge. It was his favourite breakfast and he settled down to *The Times Crossword*. The top left-hand clue was 'Devils yield to temptation, sacrificing maiden on island.' (7) Oh dear! Move on to the next clue. 'It's very bad, so a dog said.' (9) Try a clue down. 'Mothered in an evil way, we hear?' (6) Lancelyn threw the newspaper away from him in disgust and fear. SUCCUBI, ACCURSED, DAMNED. So he was, accursed and damned, first by women and then by words, books and literature. Looking sightlessly down on the porridge, he announced to the empty kitchen, 'I'll burn my books.'

Yes, it was the least he could do for love of Molly. He prepared himself mentally for this ultimate act of abnegation by rising and walking slowly to the library. Molly was beautiful and good, whereas the library was a monster, endlessly seeking to grow and in search of forbidden knowledge. It was a living hive mind with swarm intelligence. Its volumes, furious at the prospect of being jilted in favour of a woman, rippled before his eyes and cried out to him, 'WE ALL HATE YOU TO DEATH.' Lancelyn was careful to stand in the middle of the room. He had read of scholars being killed by falling bookcases. Rabbi Aryeh of Metz had been killed by a bookcase that was full of the works of authors with whom he had quarrelled. But why, he asked himself, why does the library hate me? Those winds of eternity were blowing through the library, blowing through everything. A bright red succession of books seemed to stream down from shelf to shelf until they reached the floor. It was hard to see the way out. This was no less absurd than the dream of M.R. James and Iron Foot Jack. He could not be haunted by similes and metaphors. No one had ever died of the pathetic fallacy.

He hurried away. He would burn as many of his books as he could manage in the back garden. It would be like a Viking funeral, for his books, arranged as his bed, should furnish his pyre. Molly would be pleased. But first he needed something to make the books burn. Taking the glove puppet with him for company, he hurried out to the ironmonger's store where he bought a large can of paraffin. The can was heavy, so he thought that he would stop for a rest in the staff common room. He entered with the can in one hand and the glove puppet on the other. He got some curious looks, but he promptly seated himself opposite Quentin, who took the can and put it carefully to one side and looked at what Lancelyn had on his other hand. Then he cried out cheerfully, 'Why it's Sooty!'

Lancelyn looked doubtfully at his hand, before replying, 'Talk to the glove puppet.'

'Sooty is his name,' Quentin added helpfully. (How did Quentin know so much stuff?) 'But why can't I talk to you?'

'It is no use talking to me. Talk to Sooty if you must, because otherwise you would be addressing your remarks to a dead man. Look at these fungal brown spots on my arms and hands. I caught foxing from my books and now my whole body is foxing and putrefying. You can smell it. It is like being buried alive… except it is the opposite of that, since I am dead, but unburied. Dead and haunting myself. No, I don't want a sandwich. Cremation seems best. I no longer need to eat. Cobwebs cover my face though I keep brushing them off, except that it is not my face. It is that of an impostor.'

Quentin looked baffled. Then he cried out, 'That's Cotard's Syndrome!' Though he was at first triumphant, his face rapidly clouded. 'Stay here Sooty, and look after him while I make a phone call. Don't move. I will only be a minute.'

Lancelyn shouted after him, 'Is this syndrome something that dead people get?'

But by then Quentin was out of earshot. He did come back quickly and started talking so fast that he was almost gabbling. Was Quentin going mad? He started talking about agalmatophilia which was sexual attraction to dolls. Also did Lancelyn know about maschalagmia, which was sexual attraction to armpits? And so on. In Quentin's universe everybody seemed to be the victim of big words. Where did he get his words from? Perhaps 'It Pays to Increase Your Power' in *The Reader's Digest*. Then two men turned up and they courteously persuaded Lancelyn to leave the common room and come with them. He could not understand why he had to leave the paraffin behind. The men only re-donned their white coats once they were inside the ambulance. Lancelyn had been expecting a hearse, but he supposed that an ambulance would do to take him to the undertaker. He congratulated himself, for it was not everybody who got to experience being driven to his own funeral. He wondered if Molly would be at the service. The answer had to be yes!

Everybody remembers where they were on the day Kennedy was killed. Lancelyn was in the patient's lounge of the Swansdown Home. He had not been particularly interested in the assassination, but he happened to remember that day because it was the day that he caught a glimpse of Sooty on television. So Sooty really was famous! At first Lancelyn had been incarcerated in a large mental hospital in Dundee. His parents soon got him moved to Swansdown, a private sanatorium in the south of England. (Sadly Sooty got lost in the move.) Lancelyn had been a placid patient. It had been like walking away from a car crash in a dazed state of shock.

CHAPTER TWENTY-THREE

That was all so long ago. So many years on Lancelyn continued to do the crossword and look for omens in the clues in a kind of *Sortes Virgilianae*. Today 'Confused analogist?' (8) summoned up nostalgia and led him to reflect on its very sweet pain.

> 'And youth will still be in our faces,
> When we cheer for the Eton crew.'

They had all been so young and mad, except of course for Raven and Wormsley who had been old and mad. Now he thought about it, there was a kind of symmetry in the matching of his and Molly's youthful madness with Raven's dementia. But so much fuss about nothing very much! One thinks that someone is going to be important in one's life, but then he or she just isn't and that person drops out of sight. That was what happened to Bernard. He vanished. People do vanish. A thorough internet search by one of Marcus' geekish underlings revealed nothing. Marcus, prior to retirement, had been very grand in whichever television company he had worked for – or rather whichever television company had worked for him.

Molly was not so very important either. Lancelyn had no idea how or when she and Jaimie broke up. He reportedly stayed on in the department and eventually became a senior lecturer. True to his word, he never published *The World of Fiona MacAlpine*. Molly, on the other hand, did publish a briefly successful novel. *The Rod* was about domestic cruelty. He gathered from a review that two Oxford twits appeared in the book, though they were not important characters. Even so, perhaps Bernard would be pleased, if he was still alive. He had always wanted to be in a novel. Lancelyn had never read Molly's one. He never read books by women, nor for that matter novels about serious social issues. He was currently reading a terrific thriller by Lee Child called *Killing Floor*. These days Lee Child was far more famous than Walter de la Mare. Molly had lived with a poet and later committed suicide. Or was it the woman in the novel who committed suicide, while in real life the poet she lived with who killed himself? Lancelyn could no longer remember. Wormsley died of a heart attack before he could launch a creative writing programme in St Andrews. Whereas Lancelyn had lived on to see the nastiness of futurity: those awful mobile phones, plastic water-bottles, e-readers, computers and twerking.

Tempora mutantur et nos mutamur in illis. After one's

youth, the rest of life is a biological and spiritual afterthought. As someone remarked in one of de la Mare's ghost stories, 'What is anybody's life, sir, come past the gaiety of youth, but marking time?' Then of course there was Conrad, 'Tell me, wasn't that the best time, that time when we were young… and sometimes a chance to feel your strength – that only – what you all regret!' And yet, Lancelyn, like Raven, believed that he no longer had anything in common with the youth that had occupied his sex-propelled body in the early sixties.

The sun of late afternoon had brought out the yellow and violet shades of the distant vegetation. Why does the natural world need to be so beautiful? Looking across the water to the trees of Juan-les-Pins, Lancelyn reflected that what happened during the years of one's youth and the subsequent accelerated advance towards old age would matter so very little compared with the eternity that lay ahead. His books had sold at auction for a surprising amount of money. He took some pride in that. It had to be true that there are no proper climaxes in real life. Though seemingly so important and exciting, it really drifts on like a badly ordered dream. He could just hear one of Charles Trenet's songs playing below. Then Sylvie came up on deck bearing drinks.

THE END

The Arabian Nightmare – Robert Irwin

'Robert Irwin is indeed particularly brilliant. He takes the story-within-a-story technique of the Arab storyteller a stage further, so that a tangle of dreams and imaginings becomes part of the narrative fabric. The prose is discriminating and, beauty of all beauties, the book is constantly entertaining.'

Hilary Bailey in *The Guardian*

'...a classic orientalist fantasy tells the story of Balian of Norwich and his misadventures in a labyrinthine Cairo at the time of the Mamelukes. Steamy, exotic and ingenious, it is a boxes-within-boxes tale featuring such characters as Yoll, the Storyteller, Fatima the Deathly and the Father of Cats. It is a compelling meditation on reality and illusion, as well as on Arabian Nights-style storytelling. At its elusive centre lies the affliction of the Arabian Nightmare: a dream of infinite suffering that can never be remembered on waking, and might almost have happened to somebody else.'

Phil Baker in *The Sunday Times*

'Robert Irwin's novel *The Arabian Nightmare* was one of my favourite books of the early 1980s and one of the finest fantasies of the last century.'

Neil Gaiman in *Authors at Christmas*

'Robert Irwin writes beautifully and is dauntingly clever but the stunning thing about him is his originality. Robert Irwin's work, while rendered in the strictest, simplest and most elegant prose, defies definition. All that can be said is that it is a bit like a mingling of *The Thousand and One Nights* and *The Name of the Rose*. It is also magical, bizarre and frightening.'

Ruth Rendell

£9.99   ISBN 978 1 912868 62 9   266p   B. Format

The Limits of Vision – Robert Irwin

'Very funny: it sparkles with brilliance and has a truly superb ending. I confidently predict that there will never be a better novel about housework.' *The Fantasy Review*

'Irwin is an irrepressibly clever writer but never irritating. The book binds together philosophy and mayhem. *The Limits of Vision* ranks as a genuine (and rare) work of the imagination.' Jeanette Winterson

'…unique, a ravishing product of pure imagination.'
The New Statesman

'Terrorised by the imminent arrival of her coffee-morning ladies, she vacuums the carpet, only to be bested by the spirit Mucor, whose Latin name embodies all elements of slime and grime and who tries to entice her into the kingdom of filth over which he rules. To avoid him she enters the dazzling cleanliness of the Pieter de Hooch canvas hanging on her wall, invoking de Hooch and a raft of other geniuses – Darwin, Teilhard de Chardin, Leonardo, Blake, Dostoyevski, even Jesus to assist her. The coffee-morning ladies arrive; she half-listens to their prattle while impatiently waiting for them to leave so she can attack the dishes they have dirtied. Soon her husband, whom she suspects of having an affair with one of the ladies, will come home; how can she defeat Mucor before that moment? The solution is in perfect harmony with this astonishing work of imagination and erudition.' *Kirkus Reviews*

The Limits of Vision has recently been made into an animated film by US filmmaker Laura Harrison.

£8.99   ISBN   978 1912868 57 5   120p   B. Format

Satan Wants Me – Robert Irwin

'Irwin is a writer of immense subtlety and craftmanship, and offers us a vivid and utterly convincing portrait of life on the loopier fringes of the Sixties. *Satan Wants Me* is black, compulsive and very, very funny.'

Christopher Hart in *The Daily Telegraph*

'Part of the book's fertile comedy stems from the ironic interweaving of the jargons of sociology, hippiedom and magick. It is hard to resist a pot-head mystic who hopes the Apocalypse will come on Wednesday because it will break up the week.' Tom Deveson in *The Sunday Times*

'Robert Irwin's *Satan Wants Me* was a mad confection of black magic and 60s sexual liberation, a paranoid fantasy that drew heavily on the legacy of Aleister Crowley, but achieved a wonderful lightness of touch.'

Alex Clark in *The Guardian's Books of the Year*

'Pulsing with lurid detail and swarming with perverse characters – Aleister Crowley, Rimbaud and Janis Joplin all flit past – Irwin's erudite, sabre-sharp novel closes the gap between psychedelia and psychosis. A bad trip but a great journey.' Victoria Segal in *The Times*

£9.99 ISBN 978 1 912868 20 9 320p B. Format

Exquisite Corpse – Robert Irwin

'Robert Irwin's spectacular intense novel of love and madness among the provincial British surrealist movement works all the better because authentic factual detail is woven so effectively into the fancy.'   Roz Kaveney in *The New Statesman*

'The final chapter of the novel reads like a realistic epilogue to the book, but may instead be a hypnogogic illusion, which in turn casts doubt on many other events in the novel. Is Caroline merely a typist from Putney or the very vampire of Surrealism? It's for the reader to decide.'

Steven Moore in *The Washington Post*

'Robert Irwin is a master of the surreal imagination. Historical figures such as Aleister Crowley and Paul Eluard vie with fictional characters in an extended surrealist game, which, like the movement itself, is full of astonishing insights and hilarious pretensions. Superb.'

Ian Critchley in *The Sunday Times*

'*Exquisite Corpse* is one of the best novels I have read by an English person in my reading time. When I first read it I was completely bowled over.'

A.S. Byatt on *Radio 4's Saturday Review*

£8.99   ISBN 978 1 907650 54 3   249p   B. Format

My Life is Like a Fairy Tale – Robert Irwin

'Robert Irwin vividly and brilliantly blends the fictional life and all-too-real times of a film star of the Nazi era in this a narrative of diminishing options and the advance to death and destruction. Cultured, clever and funny at times, in a grim Charles Adams way, Robert Irwin's novel is engrossing and enveloping. From a dull Dutch childhood in Dordrecht and a waitressing job, sexy Sonja Heda, cigarette in hand, wangles her way on to the film sets of various independent production companies making the films of the Weimar and Nazi eras. From *The Blue Angel*, *The Gypsy Baron*, *Jew Suss*, *Habanera* and *Munchausen* she lands the starring role in the Nazi screwball comedy *Bagdad Capers*. Although German cinema became a key part of the Nazi war effort, the film industry continued to produce commercial films appealing to the varying film tastes of German filmgoers. Joseph Goebbels at the head of the Ministry of Propaganda propagated Nazi supremacist ideology and indoctrinate the population of Germany though film and radio, not unlike the way reality TV and social media are used today by populist politicians in the US and UK.'

Georgia de Chamberet in *Ten Books for Independent Minds*
from *Bookblast*

'An entertaining romp through early German cinema as well as a multi-layered examination on the nature of storytelling that has a warning for us all. Another masterpiece from Robert Irwin.'   *The Digital Fix*

£11.99   ISBN 978 1 912868 19 3   350p   B. Format

Wonders Will Never Cease – Robert Irwin

'Robert Irwin's latest novel has much in common with *The Game of Thrones*. Both are based on the gory struggle of the Wars of the Roses, both inject large amounts of magic and the occult into their narratives, and both are hugely enjoyable, fast-moving and filled with dark humour. Though Irwin uses the actual events of York versus Lancaster in 15th-century England, he is happy to change things to make a better story – and how stories are created, recycled, embellished and interact with reality is at the heart of the book. It comprises a palimpsest of fables, myths, legends, romances, chronicles and sagas.

His hero is Anthony, Lord Scales, brother to the beautiful Elizabeth who becomes Edward IV's queen, and one of the Woodville clan whose rapid and resented rise is one motor of the mayhem unleashed by these titled gangsters. We meet him first at the battle of Towton, the bloodiest in English history, where he is apparently killed. After three days of strange encounters in a limbo landscape he returns to life and continues on picaresque adventures of chivalry and horror. Often bewildered, often slipping into occult spaces, he meets people like Sir Thomas Malory, author of *Le Morte d'Arthur*, and the alchemist Ripley (believe it or not) who turns Anthony's life into a legend. As one character observes: "The real world is a poor thing compared to the stories that are told about it."'

Ian Irvine in *Prospect Magazine*

'Amply researched yet unceasingly insistent on its own fictionality, Irwin's latest novel is like an intricate medieval tapestry or multicoloured stained-glass window, promising neither truth nor falsehood, only wonder... Irwin has brilliantly refashioned medieval history as a myth for our own time.'

Andrew Crumey in *The Literary Review*

£9.99 ISBN 978 1 910213 47 6 392p B. Format